To Corey

The Legend of Loftus Hall

Chris Rush

What if it's true?

ISBN-10: 1722170077
ISBN-13: 978-1722170073

A note from the Author

The Legend of Loftus Hall is a work of fiction based on the legend associated with the building and the relevant people during that era. To create this story, many elements had to be added to achieve the narrative and is not intended to be, and should not be taken literally. This work is not stating that the actions within its pages are those of the individuals at the time. This work reflects how Loftus Hall's structure was laid out at the date of publication and is not by any means a history book.

I want to thank Aidan Quigley, owner of Loftus Hall, for the opportunity to write this story and for his valuable knowledge and input throughout the duration of the project.

Acknowledgements

I want to firstly thank you, the reader, for reading my
work.
A huge thanks to Aidan Quigley for asking me to write
The Legend of Loftus Hall.
Thanks to all my family and friends for your continued
support.
I want to thank Billy Cullen for his work on producing a
brilliant cover.
I also want to mention Talina Perkins who formatted the
cover design for publishing.
A final thanks to my good friend Lisa V. Proulx who
edited this book for me.

"You'll never rid this place of me priest, I am eternal." The dark stranger.

Chapter 1

Darkness descended across the Hook Peninsula as the flurrying gusts of wind beat their way over the flat landscape. It was summer, however the weather that night would have made one think they were stepping out into the grasp of the harshest winter night. The waves continued to thrash against the jagged shoreline, and the only sign of life was the flickering candle light illuminating from the numerous, huge windows of Loftus Hall.

Loftus Hall was a massive, imposing three story building, which, even at a glance commanded respect. From its large stone walls entering the grounds, to its unforgettable pair of eagles perched proudly above the main door, it was a landmark like no other, standing defiantly against all Mother Nature could throw at it.

Within the building, screams of agony echoed through its long corridors, as servants scurried to and from a room on the middle floor with towels and bowls of water. Inside the chamber lay Anne Loftus, wife of Charles.

"Oh God!" she bellowed, face grimacing as another dart of pain sprinted its way through her body.

Standing, watching from her beside was her husband, a member of the Tottenham family.

"Come on, come on, hurry up," he spat to the next servant who entered the room, hoping the next supply of fresh towels splashed with cold water over her forehead, would silence her screams.

Charles was a proud and somewhat arrogant man who demonstrated his authority every chance he got. He took no prisoners which was evident by the responsiveness of the servants to his commands, fearing any reprimand from the man who gave them their living.

Hours had passed since Anne's water broke and with every release of agony, it seemed to be getting louder, even damping out the relentless winds outside.

"Okay, the baby is coming now," the doctor announced at the foot of the bed.

"Charles," Anne said, reaching her hand out to his.

Quickly he took it, hoping the relentless shrieking would be over soon.

Minutes later, the doctor had a baby girl in his hands. Anne's maternal instinct instantly kicked in as she comforted her crying baby. Once in her mother's arms the sobbing stopped, except for a few short outbursts. The child's mother had lost a lot of blood, which was the next thing the doctor turned his attention to.

"More towels," he called.

"Isn't she amazing Charles? She's an angel," Anne said turning to her husband, her face now pale and fatigue taking hold of her eyes.

"She's beautiful," he replied, looking down at his daughter.

"What will we call her?"

"Why don't you decide?" Charles said.

"I've really no idea, she's so amazing," turning back to her child.

"How about Anne?" he smiled to his wife.

"Really?"

"Why not? I like that name," he said, sitting down beside his family.

Another servant entered the room with more supplies.

"Come here and say hello to little Lady Anne," her proud mother said. Charles ensured he had placed the items close to the doctor before he approached the head of the bed. "Meet the new member of the family," she continued.

The servant smiled taking in the sight of a new life having just entered the world, after exchanging best wishes, he returned to his duties.

Finally gaining control of the blood loss and checking on baby and mother, the doctor instructed the next important thing was for Anne to get some well needed rest after giving birth.

Anne Loftus was a very humble and kind lady who didn't see herself in any way above anyone else. She did indeed have land, power and riches, however she always treated everyone the same way no matter who or what they were. She was the heir to the Loftus estate and as stipulated in the family will, if she married, she was to keep her surname and her husband would have to take on the Loftus name.

Charles Loftus Tottenham was the complete opposite to Anne. He demanded the respect and privileges that came with his name and title, and living in a building such as Loftus Hall, it was easy to see the Loftus family riches had no limitations.

Each time an individual would be granted access to the Hall, it was impossible not to be awestruck by its grandeur. From the huge grounds the structure sat on, the scenic views hugging it, the three rows of nine huge windows across the front of the building, the intricate eight-pointed tiled star design on the main hall floor to the astonishing main staircase.

The main staircase was a stunning piece of hand craftsmanship which always caused deep inhales of breath. People's eyes would be drawn to the four large banisters on the main structure, the thick, curved hand rails and the sheer workmanship and dedication needed to create the magnificent designs carved within it. The main piece of the stairs consisted of fifteen steps, after which then split left and right allowing access to the middle floor of the building. Of course these were just some of the striking features which made up the splendour of Loftus Hall.

Charles and Anne had two daughters, Anne and Elizabeth. Both sisters were extremely close growing up and one of their favourite things to do was play hide and seek for hours at a time within the massive building. Another was to play out on the huge grounds when the weather permitted, and even then, Anne always made sure her daughters where wrapped in layers of clothing to protect against the harsh winds which seemed to be present more times than not.

Loftus Hall was a busy property at that time with estate dues being collected and delivered on a regular basis, however mornings always begin the same way.

Breakfast would be held in the Morning Room, a room which was entered via two huge wooden doors. The main feature of the room was the large window facing east and its purpose was to allow those inside to witness the full glory of the early morning sunrise. Anne would often sit taking in the scene unfolding in front of her with her daughters, however Charles didn't have the urge to do so. He was more concerned with the profits and privileges associated with running the estate.

When they did venture outside the grounds, the family were rarely bothered by the public from going about their routine business and they were always treated like royalty. This was due to the majority of the locals knowing the power and riches Charles had at his disposal, which transferred into opinions of them not feeling as though they were on the same level as him or his family.

One of Anne Loftus' favourite things to do once the sun decided to grace the peninsula with its warm light, was to walk the massive gardens with her daughters. She always had kind words to say to the groundskeepers and always had time to speak with each one of them they encountered.

It was a beautiful calm day as the trio inhaled the fresh sea air, Anne was doing one of her regular rounds about the property, enjoying the nature's soundtrack as the fruit trees elegantly danced in the gentle breeze.

"How big is the sea Mammy?" young Anne asked her mother as they rounded the side of the building, the gorgeous Crook Peninsula opposite them.

"Oh, where did that question come from?" she smiled. "Are you planning to go travelling away on me? I'll find you, you know," she continued, giving her a playful nudge.

Both girls giggled in reply. They enjoyed spending time with their mother and like all young minds, theirs was full of wonder, excitement, and curiosity.

"Come here," Anne said, stooping down between the pair. "You see that line over there?" pointing towards the horizon. "The sea stretches as far as the eye can see, so you could say it's bigger than the very land we walk on. Now don't you go journeying around the world on me you hear?" she then threw her arms around the pair and began tickling them.

"Mammy," the pair rapidly chuckled, trying to catch their breath.

Breaking free, the pair ran in an effort to get away from their mother who had more spontaneous giggles in store for them. From a distance, it was evident the amount of love Anne had for her daughters.

"Careful of that pond now girls," she shouted after them standing to her feet. She had often warned them to stay away from the sump area at the side of the building, opposite the Tapestry Room. During heavy, continuous rain, this area would fill up and hold water within it for some time before draining away.

Cheerful squeals filled the air, knowing their mother was hot on their tail. Catching up on them without any difficultly, she latched onto them and pulled them down onto the soft green, grassy blanket.

"I've got you now," she said, continuing her tickling bombardment.

All the girls could do was laugh, struggling to break free once more.

"Anne!" came a stern voice in the distance.

Charles had stepped out beneath the blue sky to ensure the Coach House was being cleaned. Having several horses on the estate meant the servants had to carry out this task on a regular basis.

"We have guests coming over this evening, how will it look if they see you like that, you don't want to get the dresses dirty now do you?" he said, rattling his head from side to side.

The family did indeed always don the very best clothing available to them and image meant everything to Charles and in his opinion, if the lady of the house was seen in dirty clothes, it wouldn't give the best impression.

In the 1700s, there were not many ways to help take the boredom out of long nights, so Charles and Anne would regularly invite friends over to play cards to pass the long dreary evenings.

"Okay girls, let's go inside," she said, helping them to their feet, brushing the loose grass off their dresses and her own before passing Charles inside the house.

Later that evening, laughter echoed from the Card Room whilst the servants where venturing back and forth with large glasses of wine and whiskey. Playing cards seemed to be a very thirsty game indeed. The guests had been there quite some time and the game was in full swing. After tucking the girls into bed upstairs, Anne stepped down the main staircase, aided by the flickering candles throwing their light from atop the banisters, entered the Card Room, and took her set at the table.

"I'm glad you're back dear, they are destroying me," Charles said, taking a swig of whiskey from his glass and dealing out of the pack once more.

Anne smiled across the table to the others as the dancing flames within the fireplace gently heated her back, "I don't know if I'll be able to change that."

At the grand table, which the group were playing cards on, stood a single candle, and it sat beside one of two large windows in the room. Even though the thick, heavy red curtains where drawn, a slight chill could be felt making its way around the room, so the warmth from the fire was a welcome feeling.

"I don't believe it," Charles said, losing again. One thing which didn't sit nicely with him. After all, he was the Lord of the House and had to give the impression of being strong and a *winner*.

"Okay, let's go again," he instructed, finishing his drink. "Whiskey!" he shouted, dealing the cards around the table once again.

A servant quickly scurried to the table with a bottle of whiskey. "Come on, come on, fill all the empty glasses," Charles slurred, showing the effects of the alcohol he was consuming.

"Charles," Anne said.

"What? Well it is their job isn't it dear?" taking another mouthful. "Okay, let's see this time." he said, setting his cards onto the table.

Quickly glancing around the table, he noticed he had won the round. This triggered a loud cheer and a huge kiss on his wife's lips.

"Told you love, we have them where we want them," he declared.

The card game and drinking went on until the early hours of the morning until the last of the guests were walked to the door.

Once blowing out all the downstairs candles, Charles joined Anne in the children's bedroom where she was ensuring they were still in a sound slumber.

"Everything okay?" he asked, standing beside her.

"Yes, they are asleep."

"Okay, I'm going to get some rest myself," he said, and retired to bed.

Chapter 2

The sun was losing its battle with the darkness as Loftus Hall was caressed with one final ray of light. "Come on girls, dinner time," Anne shouted down the long corridor which led to the ballroom. One of the servants had beaconed the children but their mother felt that they may respond to her commands quicker.

Giggles were heard ricocheting off the walls upstairs.

"Anne, Elizabeth, come on now before it gets cold," she shouted once more towards her daughters who were now several years older, but still in their pre-teens.

Stepping down the hallway, Anne turned left and began climbing the back staircase. Which used mostly by the servants, as they weren't allowed to use the other without permission. It wasn't as spectacular as the main staircase and had far thinner handrails, but the handrail was in its own way unique, continuing from the bottom floor and curving its way all the way to the third floor. Reaching the top floor, an area where the girls would regularly play, she was instantly greeted with them running towards her.

"Careful now you," she said to Elizabeth, reaching her first, patting her on the head. "Come on you little rascals, let's get some food into those tummies," she grinned, leading both sisters back down the narrow stairs.

Reaching the last step, the enticing smell of the evening's dinner floated its way through the hall.

"Go on girls," Anne said.

A smile etching its way across her face as she witnessed the happiness of the children. Once out of sight, Anne took a deep inhale as a pain crawled its way through her midsection. She had been secretly experiencing the same discomfort on and off for a number of weeks and it was slowly getting worse. Leaning against the ice cold wall, Anne tried to regain her composure. The grimace on her face indicating the ordeal hadn't passed.

"Mammy, yours is getting cold."

"I'll be there now," she responded, quickly glancing over her shoulder to make sure no one was witnessing her distress. To Anne, it would have been a great embarrassment for anyone to see her in such a vulnerable condition, which was one of the reasons she hadn't informed anyone she was experiencing the growing pains.

Looking down at her glamorous, long sleeved, sky

blue dress, Anne knew, what she had always practiced, that her health was indeed her wealth. Exhaling slowly, she wiped her brow with the back of her hand and made her way to the dinner table to join the others.

Over the following weeks, Anne's health deteriorated further. She had begun to pass blood and the pain at night meant she was getting little or no sleep. However, she managed to keep her illness to herself. Her main concern was she didn't want to worry the girls over something she was praying would pass in time. Charles had indeed noticed his wife getting up in the middle of the night and wandering the long, dark corridors, however his concern wasn't too great. He assumed it was the occasional howling winds, whizzing through the building keeping her awake. He was a busy man concerned with upholding the influence he had obtained in the area, something which he wanted to only go in one direction.

It was a bright autumn's day when Anne Loftus collapsed aside one of the fruit trees in the beautiful gardens. She had sent the girls away with one of the servants moments before she introduced her head to the ground, sensing fatigue was finally catching up on her feeble, thinning body. One of the older servants who had been working on the estate for many years, was the first at her side.

"Miss Loftus, Miss Loftus, wake up," he said, kneeling beside her, gently shaking her about the shoulders.

There was no response.

"Help!" he roared.

Within moments, other servants were around Anne, watching in shock as they observed her grow paler with each passing second.

"Let's bring her inside," the older servant instructed the others.

Charles arrived home later that evening and by then a local doctor had been sought to attend and examine Anne.

"What's wrong with her?" he asked, as the doctor closed the bedroom door behind him. Charles had just enough time to eye Anne's sleeping, skeletal face illuminated by the flickering candle light, as confusion worked its way through him.

"I don't know, but she is extremely ill. I don't think she has long Charles," was the shock inducing response.

"I knew she wasn't eating a lot of late and had lost quite a bit of weight, but I didn't think it was this bad," Charles said, trying to source and portray the suitable emotional response.

"You should prepare for the worst at this stage, she told me she has been suffering pains, tiredness, excessive sweating during the night, and severe weight loss. As far as I can tell, she is slowly dying,"

"Can we do anything?" Charles spouted.

"There is really nothing we can do I'm afraid. Symptoms like she is displaying point to one possible cause. In my opinion, it's a developing cancer Charles, it's gradually killing her," the man placed a hand on the Lord of the house's shoulder, "Spend time with her, she wants to see the girls too."

Watching the slim man walk from him, Charles's mind was bombarded with questions. This was something he didn't see coming and he wondered what would happen if his wife did indeed die.

For instantly thinking of himself first, guilt slithered its way through his head as he closed the heavy door behind him, and walked towards his dying wife.

"I'm dying, aren't I?" Anne coughed, trying to rest herself in the bed.

"I don't know what to say but yes, yes you are," the words fell from his mouth with a deep sigh. He couldn't believe he was saying such a thing to her.

"Do the children know?"

"I don't think so, I haven't seen them yet," he responded, placing a hand on hers.

"Can you go get them for me?" she asked pulling away, "I want to speak with them before I get any worse."

Charles did as he was asked and fetched Anne and Elizabeth. Both girls entered the room teary-eyed and afraid, never before had they seen their beautiful mother in such a helpless condition.

"Come here, it's okay," she said to the distraught pair, beckoning them over to her bedside.

"What's wrong Mammy?" Elizabeth asked. "Are you going to be okay?" her sister quickly added. Both studying every detail of their mother's deteriorating face.

"I'm okay girls, don't you worry about me," she released a flurry of agonising coughs. "Did you get up to anything interesting this evening?"

"We don't want to lose you," Anne said, erupting into heart wrenching sobbing.

This trigged the same reaction from Elizabeth.

"Hey, come here you two. I am never going to leave you okay. I'll always be in here," Anne said, pointing towards her heart, "Never forget that."

The children remained at their mother's side all evening, until they finally succumbed to tiredness and she asked them to lay in the bed beside her. She didn't sleep for some time. The dying woman looked at her beautiful children wondering why she had to leave them so early in their lives. She was unable to distinguish which hurt more, the thoughts of not being there for them as they grew up, or the cancer slowly pushing its way through her body.

Over the next number of days, Anne regained a fraction of her strength and pulled her aching body from the bed. She was a proud lady and while she still had breath in her lungs and strength in her legs, she wasn't going to see out the remainder of her days lying in a bed staring at a ceiling.

Using a walking aid left by the doctor, she negotiated her way down the main staircase, using its huge handrails to support her weight, stepped through the Card Room into the main hall and exited the front door. Instantly, the crisp sea air filled her lungs whilst she enjoyed the occasional whistling and cawing of the birds overhead. Yearning for one last walk around the estate while she still had the mobility to do so, she stepped down into the grand gardens. Once spotted, two of the groundskeepers rushed to her side.

"Thank you," she said as they each linked an arm.

"Mammy!" she heard through a joyous shout.

Looking left, she saw her beloved daughters running towards her, wide eyed, each displaying a massive smile of excitement seeing their mother out and about.

"How are you girls?" she asked, wrapping her left arm around them both.

"You're getting better," young Anne said with her head pressed firmly against her, as she hugged her mother.

"A little," was the reply.

However deep down she knew it was only a matter of time before the inevitable occurred.

Anne spent the whole morning slowly ambling the grounds with her daughters, taking in what she knew could quite possibly be her last time to do so. Stepping from the walled gardens, a smile etched its way across her face. Although in immense pain and suffering heart ache, knowing she wouldn't be a part of her children's lives for much longer. At that moment, looking at them enjoy her company as much as she did theirs, it warmed her soul.

Arriving down the long avenue to Loftus Hall, Charles spotted Anne, who was still being supported by the men who had helped her to relish her morning so perfectly.

"Shouldn't you be resting?" he said reaching the group.

"I'd rather be out here," she quickly returned.

"Are you sure you're able to do be doing this? It could put a lot of strain on you," Charles continued.

"Listen, don't worry about me I'll be fine. I'm just going to spend a little more time out here and then I'll be going back to bed,"

Charles didn't attempt to persuade her any further and accompanied his family for a walk down towards the sea. Staring out at the horizon and then across to Crook Head, Anne turned to her children and said,

"It will always be beautiful, but it will never come close to the both of you,"

The sisters smiled in response.

Satisfied, Anne returned to the house where she spent the remainder of the day and evening sitting beside the warm fireplace in the Morning Room watching the hustle and bustle of the daily chores being completed around her.

After joining the family for evening dinner, at which she could only manage a sip of water, Anne decided to return to her bed. She was offered help, but refused. She was determined to keep her independence right until the end.

Ascending the stairs, the majority of which was now shrouded in darkness, except for the areas illuminated by the flickering candles trying to fight it back, Anne knew that soon she would close her eyes and never open them again. She smiled hearing the girl's laughter echoing up the stairs behind her, the sound hugged her with a pleasant feeling. It lifted their mood seeing her on her feet earlier that day, something which she was thankful for. The last thing she wanted to do was die knowing that for the last few days she shared the same air as them, they were grieving and reluctant to come near her for fear of hurting her delicate body, instead of enjoying the last time they had together. *The grieving process should come afterwards,* she thought.

Blowing out the bedside candle, Anne slowly eased herself down onto the blankets, taking in a few deep inhales as she did. That day had been a good day for her and one of which she was thankful she had had the time to do.

That was the last time Anne Loftus would be able to move about the Hall on her own again.

Chapter 3

Two long, pain induced weeks crawled by as Anne slowly deteriorated into a bed ridden fossil of her former self. Her cries of agony during the day and night hours were so deafening they drowned out the waves crashing against the shore. It had reached the stage where literally any movement at all sent a slice of pain shooting through her.

Occasionally, during the early hours of the morning, she would spot the two sisters standing in the doorway, looking at her attempts to toss and turn for some sliver of unattainable comfort. Of course she would put on a brave face and call them inside. After reassuring them everything would be okay and kissed them goodnight, young Anne and Elizabeth would return to their beds, only to repeat the same process the following night.

Observing the impact her illness was having on her family's emotions, she called Charles to her chamber on a heavily overcast afternoon.

"I can't do this Charles," she said as he sat down beside her.

"I can't even imagine the pain you must be going

through,"

"It's nothing compared to the distress I see on the girl's faces each time they walk in through that door. I can't bear to see them so upset Charles," wincing, raising herself up slightly beneath the heavy blankets, "I don't want them watching me slowly die in front of them,"

"I don't understand."

"I don't want their last memories of me to be howls of agony and slowly growing paler and thinner with each passing day." She finished as the tears began to flow down her face past her dry lips.

Both Anne and Charles decided the local doctor should be contacted again, who was already carrying out examinations on Anne every morning to assess her health. He arrived again later that afternoon. Following a quick examination, he returned to the hallway where Charles was waiting. Closing the door behind him, he gently shook his head towards Charles, indicating the news wasn't going to be any better than what he had given earlier that day.

"It's only a matter of days," he said. "She told me about her concerns with your daughters and my mind would never be at ease if I couldn't help her pass as comfortable as possible."

Charles scrunched his eyebrows wondering where

the conversation was going.

"I have a guest house beside my own. I offered to move her there so the children's visits could be scheduled when she feels she will be up to it and keep their minds as well as her own at ease. I did mention to her that she might miss them freely coming and going from her room, but she is determined this is the best way to cause them the least amount of anguish as possible. I informed her the move would be extremely painful, but she has agreed this is what she wants. She wants to die knowing they have happy memories of her."

Charles was stunned beyond words, however he agreed to the decision.

"Don't worry she will be kept comfortable and I'll have Karen check on her too."

"Will your wife mind?" Charles returned.

"Not at all, I have had a number of patients stay when they required close observation."

"Okay, I suppose if that's what she wants, we'll have to do our best for her," Charles said knowing the situation was out of his control. The thought of what would people might think knowing she had moved out of Loftus Hall shot through his mind, however he quickly cast it aside.

Anne was moved the short distance to her second last resting place the following day. Just as she was informed it was an agonising move; however, she knew the peace of mind after her ordeal would make it all worthwhile.

Michael's house sat a little over a mile away from Loftus Hall, with the small guest house at its side. Helped by Charles, the doctor lay Anne down onto the large, comfortable bed. There was no need for two men to aid her onto the bed because by then she weighed no more than a feather, however both wanted to be seen to be helping in some way.

"We'll be in and out to you, but if you need anything at all, please ring this," Michael said placing a tiny bell on the bedside table.

"Thank you," she managed to slowly exhale.

"I'll be over every day, and I'll bring the girls too once I know you're up to it," Charles added.

"Look after them and please tell them I'm fine okay?" she wheezed.

"Okay."

Anne was happier in a sense by then knowing her daughters wouldn't have to bear witness to the last breath leaving her feeble body.

She managed to cling onto life for three more days

after the move, just long enough to allow Anne and Elizabeth one final visit. They shared quite some time at the bedside before they returned to Loftus Hall and the last image they saw of their mother was her blowing them a kiss as they left the room. She passed away that evening.

When Charles broke the news to his children he couldn't decipher which cries were more heart wrenching, the wails of a dying woman or those of her grief struck daughters. He tried reassuring them they would meet their mother again someday and she had gone to a better place, but the words had no comforting quality about them. Their mother was dead and nothing could change that.

Anne's funeral was held the following week. Many people turned up to pay their respects to Lady Loftus and almost everyone broke down in the same manner once witnessing the children's despair at the graveside, and Charles trying to comfort them as much as possible. Once the last person shook his hand and told him how sorry they were for his loss, he returned home to a building he had acquired through marriage, along with its title and estate.

Charles found himself in a unique situation. He was indeed the heir to the estate now that the last line of Loftus' had passed away, the power was his. Which was one of the main enticing reasons he had married Anne in the first place, of course he never divulged this information to anyone. Indeed, he also had feelings for her and the death had had an impact on him but he was determined that life must go on and the family name could return to the right order so to speak – Charles Tottenham Loftus. The Loftus name meaning he would still have hold of the privileges which came with it.

The first number of nights without their mother were filled with continuous soft crying into their pillows. She had meant so much to them and they felt as though their life had been cruelly ripped apart and no matter how many times Charles told them everything was going to be okay, the pain only seemed to fester more.

Charles himself found it strange not having Anne around the house and to be sleeping in the grand, luxurious bedroom alone. Laying on his back, staring at the ceiling many nights, he could still hear the horrid, agonising wails as the cancer slowly ate its way through his wife. He instructed the servants to keep a close eye on Anne and Elizabeth and ensure their minds were kept as active as possible during the grieving process. Meanwhile, he maintained the upkeep of the estate and ensured the dues owed were still paid and collected on time, after all, he couldn't look weak in any way.

Over the weeks following Anne Loftus' death, life slowly retuned to some sort of routine, but to her children, life truly would never be the same again. When the weather permitted, they began to venture outdoors once more to walk about the ground of the Grand Hall. Always making sure to wrap up well and keep warm, a fond memory they both shared of their mother's love and protective nature.

The hustle and bustle on the grounds ranging from the coach house upkeep, garden maintenance and stocking fire wood etc. drew their attention from one area to another.

"I wish Mammy was here," Anne said to her sister.

"Me too."

"Do you think she is happier now? Do you think she is still in pain?" Anne continued as the cool sea air gently brushed across them.

"I really hope she is and free from the pain now," Elizabeth returned.

The pair strolled about the soil hugging Loftus Hall for quite some time remembering the happy times they had spent with their mother here. Looking out onto the old dirt road which ran adjacent to their vast land, they eyed a number of passers-by. Not one of them looked in across the old stone wall towards the dominant building.

"Have you ever noticed when most people go by,

they never lift their head?" Anne said, her inquisitive mind working overtime.

"Not really," Elizabeth giggled.

"I wonder why that is."

"Maybe we scare them," Elizabeth laughed giving her sister a playful nudge.

She ran and Anne took off after her. Reaching the beach both paused and took in the natural beauty of Crook Head, the sea carving its way between both peninsulas. The girls spent the remainder of the day down at the shoreline playing before being called for their dinner.

The candle light flickered of walls and barely stretched its way to the tall ceilings, as numerous men and women came back and forth from the kitchen with various types of food.

"Come on now girls, eat your dinner," Charles said, slurping on a big spoon full of soup.

Both did as they were told and begin to slice into their potato and meat combination. Watching the many people venture about the room Anne knew there was a seat at the head of the table, opposite her father which could never be filled again. Anne, although surrounded by many individuals, felt alone for the first time in her life. A loneliness which she knew could never be and would never be comforted again. Looking across the table at her sister, she knew she felt the exact same way.

As the weeks slowly rolled by, both children found themselves able to obtain some form of sleep during the night hours. Many of these hours were filled with the comforting dreams of their mother, which would be cruelly snatched away by the parting of their eyelids at daybreak. Charles on the other hand, found himself achieving a sound sleep a lot sooner than his children. This was due to the work he was completing to ensure the Loftus Hall estate remained a strong and formidable entity.

"This place gives me the creeps," one man told another as they walked up the long, windswept avenue towards the huge Hook Head landmark.

"Don't be silly," the other replied.

Both were arriving to give their scheduled dues to Charles for the Loftus estate.

"It's those damn birds," he said pointing towards the proud, stone, eagles perched above the main door. "I'm just waiting for them to fly down here and claw the faces off us," his eyes glued to the statues.

The other man laughed. "Don't be so damn silly,

although I don't like coming here now as much since Anne died. At least she would greet you and ask how you were doing. The other fella would barely grunt at you. Thinks he's better than us with all this money and land,"

"Let's just get this over with so we can get out of here, even the servants look at you strange coming in here."

After handing over what they owed the Loftus estate to one of Charles's representatives, they spun on their heels and quickly exited through the large stone pillars, which each boasted a stone ball delicately placed on top of them.

This was a common activity on the Hall grounds and now with Anne gone, Charles was slowly making things a lot more formal. Whatever was owed to the Loftus estate be it rent payments and so on, it had to be paid without question and always on time.

Chapter 4

A number of years passed and by then Anne Tottenham, at that stage a young woman, had no sister to confide in during the long, lonely evenings.

Elizabeth no longer lived beneath the high ceilings within the Hall. She had found love, married, and moved from the thick stone wall surroundings, to live with her husband.

On the day of her wedding, Charles gave his daughter away. Walking down the aisle, Anne spotted a number of tears escaping and trickling down Elizabeth's cheeks. Anne later finding out it was partly caused by the absence of their mother at her side. Anne recalled her sister taking her breath away on that morning. She wore a beautiful white dress which flowed effortlessly around her and jewellery fit for a queen. After the ceremony, the sisters stepped outside into the beautiful, warm sunshine and walked together for some time.

"I'm never going to be too far away," Elizabeth said, taking her sisters hand in her own.

"I know," Anne smiled, believing her sister truly meant well in her heart, but the reality would be that she would have her own life to live.

"You better come and see me you hear?"

"I will, don't worry," Anne returned, taking her sister in her arms.

"Okay, let's go and enjoy ourselves," the bride instructed, pulling her sister by the arm back to the others.

It took some adjustment for Lady Tottenham to get used to not seeing her sister around Loftus Hall. She would wonder the long corridors alone, walk the grounds alone, and spend hours in her room wondering if the day would ever come when she would experience the sense of love and happiness her sister was so fortunate to have.

By that stage in her life, Charles had in a way left her to her own devices to pass the long days about the extensive property. However, she still had the Tottenham name and would accompany him on occasion concerning family, rather estate business. When she did venture out with him, he was insistent she dress and act like the Lady she was in order to uphold the strong, proud, wealthy perception of their family name.

Charles from time to time would eye Anne

innocently chatting to local men her own age in Fethard on Sea, a village a few miles away from the great Hall. However, one scowl shot towards her from her father was enough to demonstrate his disapproval of such an act. In his eyes, none of the local families had sons who were good enough for his daughter. The Tottenham's, who now had the entire Loftus estate, were a powerful family and in Charles' strong opinion, only the best and powerful families could marry into it.

Lonely Anne always knew that in her father's eyes there would never be a man fitting for her around the area, something which made her even more forlorn. She yearned for company, friendship, and companionship. She longed for a life. Anne had grown into a beautiful young woman with long, flowing, dark hair, a slim figure and no woman for one hundred miles could compare their beauty to hers. This all being said, the only company she had was the servants who waited on her hand and foot and the walls of the building she would spend hours strolling through. Anne's only joy came from the memories her and Elizabeth shared together, but without fail, her heart would always sink knowing she would have to return to grim reality.

Maybe I should go and visit them for a while, Anne would often consider, however she didn't want to burden her sister.

Winter was fast approaching and Charles was spending more and more time away from the house on family business. Anne was spending more and more time in her bedroom watching each candle wick slowly burn to its death.

"Can I come with you Dad?" Anne asked, following him into the Main Hall and out into the front yard early one morning.

"Don't be silly dear, I'm going on important business today."

Instantly he noticed her disappointment as the glowing sunrise bounced off her equally beautiful face.

"Besides, I need to you to look after the place for me," he smiled lifting her chin back up straight. "I'll be home later, and we'll go for a walk together okay?"

She nodded in reply.

Anne knew it was an empty promise, one which she had become very well acquainted with over the last number of years. Watching him leave the property with six other individuals, Anne decided to stay out in the sunshine and try her best to enjoy the playful wildlife dancing above and around her.

Stepping into the superbly maintained walled gardens, she was bombarded by various magnificent scents concoctions being thrown about the area from the colourful flowers. Eying some of the groundskeepers at the opposite side of the garden, she made her way towards them.

"Anything I can do to help?" she asked the two individuals picking and clipping unwanted weeds within the flower beds.

"Lady Tottenham," one woman replied, scrunching her eyebrows with confusion.

"Less of the Lady," she smiled. "What can I do to help?"

Both the grubby woman and man looked at one another, each with the same puzzled looks splattered across their faces.

"Look, I'm not spending the whole day inside that place again, I need something to help me pass the time," she said, rolling up the long, glamorous sleeves on her wide white dress put together by the finest of stitching and design.

"Well, I suppose you could start with that," the woman said smiling, who couldn't be but a slight number of years older than her, pointing at the long, thin pieces of grass weaving its way through and around the flowers.

"Perfect," Anne said and began working alongside

the pair.

Soon building up a sweat, Anne paused to catch a five minute break. As the breeze caressed her flawless skin, she turned to the others,

"Do you like doing this work day in and day out?"

"Yes Lady Tottenham, we are honoured to work on such a fine estate."

"Call me Anne please," she smiled. "Where do you stay?" she wondered further. There was so many servants coming and going about the site, it was hard to keep track of who and what they did.

"We both stay in the Coach House," the man responded, wiping the sweat from his brow with the back of his hand.

"Really, do you get cold in there?" she asked, thinking of the chill that would own the Hall even with the huge fires burning within it during the night hours.

"Not so much. We sleep on the top floor you see, and the heat from the horse bedding and the horses themselves comes up through the floor and helps us keep warm during the night."

Anne was fascinated by their work ethic and their appreciation for their position on the Loftus Hall work force.

"I hope you don't mind me asking, but what has you out here with us?" the woman asked.

"I hate being in there all day long with nothing to do. It becomes so monotonous looking at the same walls for hours on end. Besides its more fun out here with you," turning back to her work, a sense of long forgotten fulfilment sweeping over her.

The trio spent the rest of day together working their way around the gardens. This had been the first instance in quite some time Anne didn't feel alone or like a piece of furniture on the property.

The sun was finally submitting to the horizon later that evening when Charles returned home. Saying farewell to the others who had accompanied him, he turned to witness his daughter helping gather and tidy away the gardening tools after her hard day's work, covered almost head to toe in dirt, her once fine, glamourous dress had patches of green and brown splotched all over it.

"What the hell are you doing?" Charles shot at her.

"Father I was-"

"And you, are you not able to do your own work without having someone to help you do it?" he fired towards the pair Anne had happily lent her assistance to for the day.

Looking at her father, she witnessed a man who was truly angry at what he had come home to, she had only ever seen him like this when his reputation could be affected.

"Get inside," he instructed.

"But-"

"Now!"

Anne threw a tiny smile and nod to her new found friends and did as instructed. Meanwhile her father stayed behind staring a hole through the pair.

"If I ever and I mean *ever*, see either of you talking to my daughter again I will have you both out of here so quick you won't know what hit you. Do you understand?"

"Yes sir," came the quick response.

"Sorry?" he returned, raising his voice, eyes glaring.

"Yes Mr. Tottenham."

"Good, now get back to work before I change my mind,"

Turning on his heels, Charles followed Anne into the building which was slowly being engulfed in darkness. Following the faint sobbing through the

Card Room, he found his daughter in the Drawing Room sitting beside one of the windows.

"Leave me alone," she said spotting him coming towards her.

"Don't you dare speak to me like that," he said pulling her hands abruptly from her face. "Do you want to tell me what you thought you were doing out there today?"

"I was only trying to help," Anne said looking at his feet.

"Help?" He roared, "The Tottenham's don't help servants under any circumstances do you understand?"

Charles awaited an answer but the only response he was getting was the continued weeping in front of him.

"How do you think that would have looked to all the other workers here today and to anyone who may have walked by? Have you any idea how much work I put in to uphold our powerful reputation, so others will respect us and then you do this?" he snarled.

"I don't care about any of that, I feel so alone in this place. I just need someone to talk to, so that's why I went out there today, what do you expect me to do?" she said taking in deep inhales.

"Don't give me that. You're the lady of this house and I never want to see you working or associating with those people ever again okay? And don't give me that loneliness nonsense, have you any idea the amount of people who would kill to be in your position? So snap out of it and grow up!"

"If Mum was here-"

"She's dead. Now get changed and clean yourself. I have guests coming over later to play cards and you'll be there too,"

Charles turned and stormed from the room, leaving Anne staring out into the darkness. She was completely stunned by her father's reaction and didn't wish to face his wrath any further that evening, so she climbed to her feet and went to wash herself.

Sitting in her bedroom, daydreaming into the mirror as she brushed her long flowing hair, she thought of her mother. If she was still alive, there would have been no chance her father would have treated her in such a way. Furthermore, her heart wouldn't be experiencing the creeping, aching isolation which was slowly consuming her.

Watching the shadows bouncing about the room in the reflection, she could hear the laughter echoing from the Card Room. Her father's guests had arrived and had already began their game and drinking. Sighing deeply, she knew she would have to endure the next number of hours pretending to be interested in their conversations and laugh at their stupid jokes.

Entering the room, she eyed five men, including Charles, seated comfortably at the table flinging cards about and slurping on their large glasses of alcohol. The Card Room was alive with candle flames and to one side stood the servants, hands clasped, patiently awaiting their call to action.

"Come on dear, join us," Charles said, spotting Anne standing within the large doorway.

He has changed his tune as usual when there is an audience, she thought.

"Anne," he continued.

Re-enacting her best fake smile, she nodded and crossed the floor and took her seat beside her father. Charles was once again putting on a strong front, displaying that theirs was a united, happy family, one of which granted an audience to a very lucky select few friends.

"So, when are you going to give us all a day out?" one of the men, whose name escaped Anne, asked her.

Anne give no response, seclusion was clogging her

throat. She yearned for love but didn't know where to find it.

"It'll take a fine fellow to steal Anne's heart," Charles finally said, breaking the awkward silence.

Hearing these words, Anne threw another false smile around the table, even though deep down all she wanted to do was explode into a torrent of tears due to the isolation she was feeling within and around the huge walls of Loftus Hall.

"Thanks for having us Charles," slurred one of the intoxicated men as they departed down the long, dark path leading from the grounds, in the early hours of the following morning.

Turning, the man of the house witnessed his daughter walking away from him to her bedroom.

Closing the large door behind her, she walked to her bed, sat on its side and began to sob softly into the palms of her hands. She was convinced life itself was making a mockery of her. She had experienced so much happiness in the house when her mother was alive and well, and then she was cruelly and painfully taken away from her. Then there was her sister who had found love and left the house. This was something which Anne was truly happy about but it also meant she now had no one to confide in on nights such as the one she was currently experiencing. She thought about how her father had treated her earlier that day and wondered if she would ever find her true love. Surrendering to tiredness, Anne lay down on the bed and listened to the waves softly beat off the shore a short distance away. Eventually she drifted off to sleep which seemed to be the only piece of comfort the young Lady could get from life.

The months rolled by and the monotony of her daily life was slowly breaking her down. Charles was staying away for days at a time now and her only company was the people who worked for them, whom had been firmly warned by her father and by then afraid to put a foot wrong in Anne's presence. Anne indeed did bump into the pair she had helped in the garden the day her father had lost his temper, while she was taking one of her many walks about the Hall. When she displayed one of her rare, genuine smiles, the pair just turned, each picked up a basket of laundry and walked in the opposite direction.

It was a dark, gloomy Friday night when Charles returned home. He had been away on family business since the previous Wednesday morning and had not returned to Loftus Hall alone. Anne was already in bed and didn't bother getting up to greet her father. In her mind, he clearly was happier making a name for himself than worrying about her, so why should she worry about him.

Hearing the flirtatious giggling emanating from the Morning Room early the next day, it was clear Charles had brought a lady friend home with him. Opening the door, Anne felt as though her heart was about to snap in two right at that very moment. Sitting across from her father, in what used to be her mother's chair, was a woman who had Charles's hand clasped in hers. She was wearing a fine, long, red dress with glorious designs throughout. Sensing Anne's presence, Charles quickly removed his hand and spun towards the doorway.

"Anne, allow me to introduce you to Jane," he said standing to his feet, left arm outstretched towards the woman who took a sip of tea before turning to her.

Dumbfounded, Anne didn't know how to respond and for a moment was convinced she was still in a sound slumber.

"Anne don't be rude now," he said stepping forward.

That movement snapped her back to reality,

"Who is *she*?"

"Jane is her name, and she's a friend,"

"A friend?" Anne said in a sarcastic tone, "So this is what's been keeping you away so much lately, did she stay here last night?"

"I'm not sure I like your tone," Charles said, his face becoming stern.

"Hello, I'm Jane," the woman said standing from the table and placing a hand before her to shake Anne's.

"So, she's moving in now is she?" Anne asked her father.

"Don't be so disrespectful," Charles instructed his daughter.

"It's okay dear," Jane said turning to him.

Hearing the sentence spoken in such a dismissive tone, as if they both were speaking to a child, was the final straw. Anne spun on her heels and stormed out of the room.

"Anne!" Her father roared after her, however she was outside within seconds.

Running to the far side of the walled gardens, Anne felt as though she had been stabbed in the heart. She couldn't believe her father could replace her mother so easily and more so, she couldn't believe this *Jane* woman had the nerve to walk into her house as if she owned the place.

"What is your problem?" Charles snapped at her

standing on the pathway which ran through the centre of the glorious gardens.

"How could you?" she said, turning to him, her face shimmering with the trickles of tears falling down her face.

"Oh grow up will you and stop making a fool of yourself. You think the world resolves around you?" He shot back, now aware they were drawing attention to themselves.

"So you can just forget her like that eh? We all don't think like you, you know," Anne said without even thinking.

"What did you say?" Charles snarled, "Get back to work!" He then growled to the grounds workers staring at the pair, who immediately did as were instructed.

Anne felt a nervousness building within her and did not wish to go toe to toe with her father as it would be a pointless attempt.

"I just really miss her Father. I'm sorry," were the words she finally managed to push from her mouth.

"You need to snap out of it Anne. You've no idea how lucky you are to be in the position you are on this estate and all you can do is go around moaning in self-pity all the time. You need to start acting your age and furthermore, who I bring to this house is my business not yours. Your mother is dead Anne, dead," he stated pointing firmly to the ground. "Now I want you to go inside and be polite like you should be and treat Jane with the respect she deserves, do you hear me?"

Anne didn't bother arguing any further, there was nothing she could do about this new woman in her father's life. So she just nodded and followed him back into the house.

Stepping back into the Morning Room, Jane had smugly retaken her seat at the table, it was clear she had made herself at home.

"Anne has something to say," Charles said, walking over to the table and sitting back down opposite Jane.

Anne couldn't believe what she was witnessing. This new woman was just strolling into their lives and dismissing her mother's memory and what made it worse, her father was helping it happen.

"I'm sorry, I shouldn't have acted like that," Anne said looking at Jane and her father sitting cosily in front of her.

"You shouldn't judge people before you get to know them," Jane said picking up her cup of tea and taking another sip. Turning to Anne, whose eyes were still struggling to contain the tears, she said, "I'm sure we will become very good friends once we get to know each other."

That statement turned Anne's stomach. She didn't want anything to do with her but judging by her father's reaction moments before, she concluded Jane was there to stay.

To appease her father, the young lady replied, "I suppose so."

Charles looked at her in a way which needed no further explanation. It was the same look he cast the evening he caught her working with the servants. His shoulders back, chest out, stern face and eyes which threw a glare of authority, one of which Anne knew she would have to obey. She would now, alongside the guests he would invite over to play cards, have to tolerate and pretend to enjoy this new woman's company.

After the pair finished their breakfast, Anne was requested to join them, as Charles gave Jane the grand tour of the house. Watching them flirt with one another made Anne sick and hearing Jane's reactions to the marvels the Hall displayed enraged her.

Some comfort warmed Anne's heart later that evening when she learned that Charles had sent word to her sister Elizabeth to come and meet the new woman in his life. Not liking the idea of someone filling her mother's shoes, the thought of seeing and being able to confide in her sister after what seemed like an eternity brought with it a snippet of happiness.

Elizabeth arrived on a glorious day the following week. Anne had been waiting for her in the doorway standing beneath the proud eagles, when she eyed her sister making her way down the long path to Loftus Hall. Instantly, the pair ran into each other's arms.

"I've missed you so, so much," Anne said, clinging onto Elizabeth.

"Me too. I told you I'm never too far away," Elizabeth smiled. "How have you been?"

Turning to see Charles waiting to introduce Jane to his other daughter, Anne decided it wasn't the best time to unload her troubles on her sister.

"Hello dear," Charles greeted Elizabeth with a kiss on the cheek. "Come on inside,"

Stepping into the house, it was like she had only left the place the day before,

"Still playing those card games eh?" she smiled, leaving the Card Room, venturing to the foot of the awe inspiring main staircase.

"Jane dear, Elizabeth is here," Charles called.

Moments later the sound of hard soled shoes echoed about the Hall. Rounding the corner, Jane appeared at the top of the stairs. She was wearing a long blue dress accompanied with white gloves. It appeared that she had settled into her new home quite easily indeed. She had developed a certain aura about her, one of which wasn't appreciated by Anne. To Anne, Jane now walked with a certain arrogance and seemed to look down upon her. The grin she bore reaching the last step did nothing, only increased Anne's disliking to her presence.

"Nice to meet you," Elizabeth said stretching out her hand.

"Well at least you didn't run away," Jane teased, taking her hand, looking towards Anne.

Confusion quickly crossed Elizabeth's face.

"But we're okay now aren't we Anne?" Jane continued.

Anne nodded in response.

"Come, let's get something to eat," Jane said, leading Elizabeth away.

It wasn't until later that afternoon when Anne and Elizabeth finally got to spend some time alone together. Doing so, they decided to take a walk like they did so many times before through the grand gardens on which the Hall sat.

"What do you think of her?" Anne said starting the conversation.

"She seems okay."

"Try living with her," Anne added.

"I'm guessing you're not her biggest fan then," Elizabeth said nudging her sister playfully.

"I just can't believe he is moving on so easily and she is walking around like she owns the place. He treats me like I'm nothing to him,"

"Listen, I know exactly where you're coming from and it can't be easy to see it happening right in front of you but my advice is to try and ignore her and concentrate on yourself. You know how Father is and by the looks of it she isn't going anywhere."

"I'm so lonely here. I've no friends. I've nothing," Anne said starting to release her sadness.

"I know you are lonely, but don't worry. The right person is out there for you too. And you do have something, you've me."

"I miss her so, so much. It's terrible living here without her."

Elizabeth took her sister in her arms.

"I know, I miss her more each day too. Remember she wouldn't even let us out here without wearing at least twenty five coats?"

"Yeah," Anne said, a smile breaking its way through the tears.

"I'm always going to be here for you, you know that right," Elizabeth stated, wiping the tears from Anne's beautiful face. "Come on let's go down to the beach," she said, taking her sister by the hand.

The pair stood at the shoreline in silence for quite some time. Each enjoying one another's company and the hypnotic sounds of the Atlantic waves gently caressing the ground they stood on.

The cawing of seagulls overhead drew their attention.

"How many times did we used to come down here?" Anne asked.

"Permitted or unpermitted?" Elizabeth said, grinning at her. Indeed, they had been good children, however like all young minds, they had a keen sense of wonderment and would sometimes venture down to the beach without their mother's consent.

Anne smiled, "We have a lot of good memories here don't we?"

"Yeah we do. I know it's hard right now but

everything will get better I promise,"

"How long will you be with us?"

"I'll be here for a few days," Elizabeth said, the joy on her sister's face indicating her delight upon hearing the words.

For the first time in weeks Anne's mood had lifted somewhat. The pair remained outdoors for the remainder of the day, and after enjoying the splendid sunset they went inside to have dinner with their father and the new lady in his life.

After three days, it was time for Elizabeth to make her way home. Anne was determined not to let her sister's departure once again upset her. She had thoroughly enjoyed the previous days, having someone to share time with and she was going to try to remain strong in hope that someday she too would make a good life for herself.

Kissing her sister on the cheek, Anne stood in the doorway until she disappeared from sight.

Closing the door behind her, she stood in the centre of the eight-pointed star and embraced the silence. Anne then closed her eyes and focused her mind. Taking deep inhales, she was determined to keep a positive outlook and try her utmost to live alongside Jane, hopeful that she would find love and make a life for herself as did Elizabeth.

"Anne!" came the stern voice from another room of the Hall.

Releasing a deep sigh, she opened her eyes, turned, and ventured back into the dark corridors of Loftus Hall.

Chapter 5

It wasn't long until Charles and Jane became man and wife. It was a grand wedding and no expense was spared. Anne's stomach churned slightly watching them each exchange the rings. Over the previous number of weeks, her relationship with her father and Jane had gone from bad to worse and her sister didn't share the same dislike for Jane as she did.

Before the marriage both sisters had the chance to talk personally again where Elizabeth revealed that she supported their father's move and was of the opinion that Jane was a nice lady. Anne, after some internal debating with herself, agreed her father was doing the right thing moving forward, as that too was her plan, however she wanted him to do it with anyone but Jane. Jane, for no clear reason to Anne, was horrible to her and never treated her with respect, in fact she was treated just like any other person who worked for the Tottenham's. Something which Charles seemed not to cast a second thought towards or was just ignoring it on purpose.

Elizabeth advised her sister she would just have to put up with whatever was going on between the pair until she found a suitable man to begin a new life with. Anne felt trapped and once again alone. By then, not even her sister could see any wrong with Jane.

After their marriage, Charles and Jane went away for a week to celebrate, leaving Anne to look after the Hall. The estate had plenty of workers and maintainers to keep it afloat, it was almost like it was its own living organism. However, for most of that time, Anne never left her room and only ventured out to eat or use the bathroom.

"We're home," Jane shouted through the main door. Charles instructing a servant to collect their belongings. "Anne!" she called.

Charles's daughter was laying on her bed when she heard the grand return, she had no interest in entertaining their reminiscing over the week just past.

"Anne," Jane once again echoed from the main hall.

Knowing she would have to face them at some stage, the young lady raised her head and ventured in the direction of the irritating voice.

"Ah there she is," Jane said spotting her rounding the corner. "Be a dear, put a fire on, and go pour us a drink, we've had a long trip,"

Anne couldn't believe what she was hearing. *Not*

even a hello, how have you been, just spouting orders the minute she walked through the door. She gritted her teeth, turned and did as she was instructed. There was no point in arguing at that stage, it would have been pointless, and she would have eventually given in and done it either way.

"How stupid are you?" Jane roared to a servant dragging one of the overloaded cases along the floor. "If you've damaged one thing in there you're out of here!"

After doing as asked, the young lady returned to her room, where for the remainder of the night she had to endure Charles and Jane's high-pitched laughter and the beckoning for more alcohol. Looking at the ceiling, she pondered where she was going to source the strength she would need to drag herself from her bed at the dawn of each day.

The weeks wore on and Jane stamped her authority further within the Hall. She had the servants running around to her beck and call and treated them as though the only useful thing they could do was mucking out the Coach House. Anytime she interacted with Anne it was with short abrupt answers and unpleasant looks which confirmed she disliked Anne just as much as she did Jane.

To Jane, Anne was an inconvenience and should have moved out of the Hall long before she and

Charles got married.

Charles by then treated his daughter little better than Jane. Jane to him was the main woman in his life by then, however to the outside world, he still portrayed them to still be the perfect family and indeed no man could just walk into Loftus Hall and snatch the truly beautiful Anne away from him without the family reputation being upheld. Not just any man would be suitable for her, he would, like Elizabeth's husband, have to come from a wealthy family and have a bright future ahead of him.

Charles began holding the card games more frequently. Anne found it harder and harder to act happy in front of the guests and she couldn't stand Jane's fake politeness and sometimes playful jokes towards her. Anne was the only individual sitting at the table who wouldn't consume alcohol, it just wasn't for her. She remembered the first time she tried it. The moment it passed her lips, she almost emptied the contents of her stomach onto the floor.

One small slice of comfort Anne seemed to get within the Hall was the warmth thrown from the fires, which fought a hard battle to keep the coldness at bay even during the summer months. The flames would burn long into the night once the winter's air cast its chilling breath across the wind beaten peninsula.

The only other ounce of enjoyment Anne seemed to get from life within the Hall was spending hours in the Tapestry Room.

The Tapestry Room, which was located to the right on the ground floor as you descended the beautiful main staircase, was a room which contained fine and elaborate tapestry works from various parts of the world. This was one way the Loftus' would demonstrate their wealth to any guests who were lucky enough to be brought on the grand tour of Loftus Hall. Many would stand in awe taking in the complex, woven thread work displaying various forms of splendid designs and images hung around the Tapestry Room walls. Some of which were gifted to the Loftus', to Charles Tottenham in later years, from other powerful families.

Anne remembered occasionally setting foot through the two large wooden doors into the room when she was younger with Elizabeth and feeling uneasy in there. "It's like stepping into another world," she once said to her sister. She also remembered overhearing many of the guests saying they didn't like the atmosphere within its walls. Charles of course put this down to jealousy and always got a kick out of bringing people there to show off items which had been gifted to the estate. An estate over which he had firm command.

Another feature proudly boasted by this ominous

room was the eight-pointed star in the centre of the ceiling which she assumed must have taken a lot of delicate craftsmanship to create and place there.

By then the Tapestry Room was used very little. Charles interests were on Jane and the estate and not many others ventured inside so Anne commandeered it to be the perfect place to spend her lonely time. She would often sit in the centre of the works, listening to the hum of the Hall alive in the background, and study every inch of thread and weave of cloth. Many times, the designs would breathe life and swirl about Lady Anne while she happily daydreamed. This was until the hustle and bustle of the servants working about the Hall brought her back to reality. A reality she wished she didn't have to experience a single moment longer.

"There you are!" Charles snarled eyeing his daughter closing the Tapestry Room door behind her. "How many times do I have to call you? Dinner is on the table, if you keep this up you'll get none."

"Sorry," is the only word Anne could push from her mouth.

A look of disgust was the only response before turning on his heels, Anne following.

Anne didn't know what was worse, being treated

like an unwanted dog or knowing that happiness was something which seemed to be nowhere within her grasp.

Chapter 6

"Anne don't be in there all day now, we've guests coming later." A voice shot in from the hallway as Jane walked down the stairs, to join Charles for breakfast in the Morning Room.

Anne couldn't have cared less at the stage but she knew it would be easier to go along with the act rather than listening to the ridicule if she didn't join them for the card game that evening.

"Seriously Charles, what is wrong with that girl?" Jane said sitting down to the grand feast of various foods laid out in front of them.

"Don't talk to me, every day she just seems to mope about the place like an old piece of furniture," he lifted a cup to his lips. "Why couldn't she be like her sister, at least she made something of herself. She better pull her socks up when I find her the right man to uphold the family name."

"Sooner the better you do. She can't stay here forever," Jane added firmly.

"I couldn't agree more," Charles returned.

Turning, Jane stared out through the huge, rain

splattered window, holding the fine diamond necklace Charles gave her between her thumb and finger. It was one of the many random gifts that he had bestowed upon her.

"It's a wild day out there isn't it," Jane said. Outside the wind howled as the waves furiously beat against the shoreline. Glancing upwards, she eyed a flock of seagulls flapping frantically against the continuing gusts. "Do you think we should cancel the game later?"

"Not at all. I'm sure it will die down by then and what would they think if we cancelled our regular card game over a small bit of stormy weather eh?" Charles grinned across to his wife.

In his opinion, if they didn't stick to their routine and cancelled over weather concerns it would show a sign of weakness. He didn't care about Mother Nature or what she threw at him and he wasn't going to let a little storm get in the way of his showing off and bragging in front of his guests.

"I suppose you're right as always," Jane playfully mocked, placing her hand atop his on the table.

"Always," Charles grinned.

After some time, Anne joined the pair at the breakfast table and so too did an awkward silence as she pushed a small portion of food and liquid into her body. The rattle of the window shutters drew her attention to the large window pane.

"Be sure to present yourself well for later won't you," Charles said with an authoritative tone. "The guests aren't coming over to see the state of you like that you know."

Anne kept staring at the environmental debris whirling about outside.

"Anne!" Charles said raising his voice,

"I know, I will," she returned.

After obtaining her fill, Anne stood from the table and left the room, leaving both Charles and Jane to mock and talk about her behind her back, not that they were afraid to do it in front of her.

For the entire day, the storm raged across the peninsula and beat against the resilient walls of Loftus Hall. Inside, various creaks and other structural stretching and swaying could be heard. Instead of easing, the gusts grew in strength so too did the ferociousness of the sea's haymakers slamming against the beach. By the time night fell, the guests were holding onto their hats walking through the main door. Welcomed by a huge warm fire and large glasses of whiskey to help heat them, the servants took their wet coats and directed them to the Card Room.

Stepping into the room, the guests were greeted by another roaring fire and numerous candles flickering about on the mantelpiece. In the centre of the grand table stood another candle enclosed in a glass frame, burning brightly.

"Come on, sit down and make yourselves at home," Charles declared stepping through the other door with a large bottle of the finest whiskeys one could get in his hand.

The three guests for the evening did as instructed. They were friends of Charles whom he often had business dealings. Johnathan, who had brought his wife Rosaline with him, pulled out a chair for her and then joined her at the table. Johnathan's brother, Francis, who himself too was a sharp business man, finished his whiskey and handed the empty glass to the servant for a refill.

"I'm feeling very lucky this week Charles," Johnathan said, picking up the deck off the table and shuffling them.

"That's what they all say," the man of the house said smirking, taking his seat opposite them.

Moments later, Anne stepped into the room. The candle light truly couldn't do her beauty its full justice, however her attractiveness was still evident due to her hypnotic, flowing dark hair and perfect features. This was verified by both Johnathan and Francis practically drooling from the mouth. She sat opposite Francis, leaving the seat to her left empty for Jane, who herself joined the table minutes later.

"How are you Anne?" Francis asked smiling across the table.

She no more wanted to be there than she wanted to speak to someone she had absolutely no interest. However, knowing the aftermath, she would be subjected to if she didn't keep up appearances, she decided to once again don her best fake smile and replied. "I'm fine thank you,"

Thankfully the cards being dealt around the table by Charles drew Francis' attention away from Anne, and so began the night's game.

The storm raged on as everyone sitting at the table, apart from Anne, became more intoxicated with every passing second. Glasses upon glasses were being scurried back and forth by the servants as Charles became louder and louder with every win that came his way. Young Lady Anne wrapped herself in an imaginary cocoon and tried her hardest to stomach the situation which she knew was all just a show to maintain the family influence and pride.

"I win again!" Charles boasted on the top of his

lungs, Jane smiling from ear to ear at his dominance at the table.

"You'll have to start going easy on us," Francis said across the table to him.

"Okay, I'll give you a chance in the next round," he grinned. "Whiskey!" He then shouted lifting up his glass.

Happy with his refill, the deal began around the table again and as it did something was approaching the peninsula from the distance.

Outside, unknown to anyone, riding atop the large crests of water was a dark ship, defiantly beating its way through the storm. Reaching Slade Harbour, the battered ship docked. Throwing a walking plank from its side, one individual emerged into the saturating darkness and stepped onto the land. Turning, the dark stranger began walking along the shoreline through the torrents of falling water. After some time, the dancing candlelight from the many windows of Loftus Hall cutting through the blackness came into sight. The lone stranger decided the Hall was the only place reachable where shelter could be sought.

The neighing of horses accompanied the loud howls of wind as the stranger strode past an open field. Turning, the caped figure reached out its hand and watched the animals gallop about furiously in a large circle. Suddenly their hooves dug hard into the ground, sending sods flying before them as they came to a halt. Moments later, one curious mare plodded through the thick mud to the individual standing at the gate, who was becoming more saturated with each passing second. Reaching the hand, the stranger petted the extremely calm horse's nose. Opening the gate, the figure climbed onto the animal's back and continued towards Loftus Hall, boldly standing proud against the bombarding elements.

After closing the large front gates, the stranger climbed back upon the horse and rode towards the enticing candlelit Hall.

A servant was attending the beautifully, tiled, main hall floor when he heard the sound of horse's hooves approaching outside. He instantly stopped his cleaning duty and stared at the door wondering who would be out on horseback at such a late hour and in the middle of a raging storm such as the one shouting its way over the land. His thoughts where quickly interrupted by three loud wraps on the external door.

The thumps were so loud, they drew Charles' attention, swinging open The Card Room door and stepping into the hall,

"What the hell are you doing out here?" he roared at the trembling servant.

The three knocks came from the door once again, Charles then realising they were coming from outside.

"Well don't just stand there, go see who it is," he instructed.

Doing as commanded, the middle-aged man took a candle in his hand, unlocked the first wooden door. Charles, who was close behind him, watched as he slowly opened the next.

Outside, standing in the unsteady candlelight, stood a tall, slim man with long dark hair, dressed head to toe in black, wearing a dark cape and hat. He had dark brown eyes and a grin which made the servant a little uneasy.

"Can we help you?" the working man stuttered.

"You can," were the words which came into the Hall in a deep voice. "I've docked at the harbour as I can't go any further due to the storm. I am wondering could I stay until it passes," The stranger's eyes glinting at the house keep.

Examining the man's attire and his demeanour, Charles was satisfied he came from a wealthy family and decided it would look extremely good in front of the others if he aided a man in such a position.

"Take his horse to the Coach House," Charles instructed.

The servant looked at him, as if to determine if he was being serious.

"Now!" Charles commanded, pointing out into the darkness.

And with that the man stepped out into the freezing rain and took the horse by its mane, instantly confused as to why there was no saddle and reins, however he didn't bother highlighting it due to Charles's manner.

"Come in my friend. We would be happy to give you shelter out of this terrible weather," he said beckoning the man into the Hall. "Sorry about that, can't seem to get good help these days," Charles added, stepping aside allowing the man to pass.

"It's quite alright."

"Come, join us. We are playing cards and you're more than welcome to play a hand if you want."

Stepping into The Card Room, the tall stranger's striking good looks instantly drew attention from the ladies.

"Whiskey!" Charles said clicking his fingers.

In the meantime he introduced the man to the others. Manners and charm seemed to ooze from him. Evident by taking the ladies hands in his and placing a soft kiss upon each of them, taking slightly longer with Anne.

"Will you join us?" Anne asked, intrigued by this new young, handsome gentlemen who had just walked into her life.

"Why not," he smiled.

"Excellent," Charles said, "Get our guest a chair."

A chair was placed at the head of the table and the man took his seat.

Anne couldn't quite put her finger on it, but there was something mysterious about him. Her cheeks turned bright crimson as she felt his eyes study her, eyes which glimmered in the candlelight, casting an unblinking stare.

Cards dealt, each player picked up their set and gazed at them.

"Beginners luck," Charles declared when the new arrival to the game won the round. "Let's go again," he said, taking a huge swig of his drink.

The cards were flung around the table and once again the dark stranger won the round.

"This isn't the first time you've played is it?" Charles grinned, gulping another mouthful of alcohol. The others slightly amused someone else was finally winning, and more so beating Charles.

"I may have played a hand once or twice, but I guess I am just lucky eh?" he said, shooting a laugh around the table, one that forced the others to join in.

Anne just smiled. Only the smile etched across her face was not a fake emotion like the many others she had displayed over the night, this smile was genuine. The man, while the others continued to laugh, fixed his eyes upon her once more and returned a grin towards her.

"You can stay until morning," Jane said to the trio as she stood from the table to go to bed. "We've plenty of rooms made up and there is no point going out into that weather at such a late hour."

Johnathan, Rosaline and Francis each took Jane up on her offer, after all, the alcohol was flowing and the fire opposite them was still burning brightly. They would also be some of the privileged who would get to spend an entire night in Loftus Hall.

Passing the man whom had come to seek shelter, Jane said,

"Just ask one of the servants to show you to a guest room when you're ready to go to bed,"

It was sometime later when the game ended and everyone decided to retire for what was left of the night.

"I can show you up if you like. There are some guest rooms on the same floor as my room," Anne said.

"Thank you dear," he said, following her.

They both ascended the grand staircase and turned left. Venturing through the corridors on the middle floor, as the storm continued to beat the countryside, Anne pointed him to his room.

"Thank you for a wonderful evening," he said taking her hand and kissing it once more.

"You're welcome," Anne said, blushing.

Stepping down to her bedroom, she turned to see him still looking at her. She smiled and watched him go inside. Closing the bedroom door behind her, she undressed and climbed into bed. Anne lay staring at the ceiling for quite some time, pondering who the strange individual was whom had come to the Hall to seek shelter. She found herself captivated by his presence and wanted to get to know him further. Eventually, sleep swept over her.

Anne awoke the following morning bright and early to the sound of laugher making its way around the Hall. She leaped from the grand bedding and scurried over to her wardrobe which contained the finest dresses money buy. Finding a beautiful black gown, decorated with gold fastens, she placed it around her slim frame. She took a hairbrush and standing in front of the large, free standing mirror, she began to make herself presentable, even though due to her natural beauty, no effect was needed. In years gone past maidens would have done this duty for her but she preferred to dress and maintain herself on her own.

Finally satisfied with her appearance, Anne made her way downstairs. Rounding the corner there was Charles, Jane, and the handsome visitor all cracking jokes with one another. She had never seen her father act in such a way with someone he had only met hours before. Her eyes widened with astonishment taking in the sight.

"Ah Anne my dear, come, join us," the man said, patting the empty chair beside him.

He wasn't wearing the black attire he had donned the night before, he was wearing fresh clothes however he still had that grin about him.

Smiling, Anne joined them at the table. Glancing outside, the winds were still battering the countryside, however, they had somewhat lessened their assault.

"How are you today Anne?" he said, pouring her a warm cup of tea.

"Such a gentleman," Jane whispered to Charles.

"Fine thank you, did you sleep well?"

"I did thank you, you?" he returned.

Before she had time to reply, Charles shot into the conversation.

"Our new friend here is going to be staying with us until the Atlantic permits him to get on his way again. We are going to give him a tour of the place after breakfast,"

"Sounds good to me," Lady Anne replied.

"Brilliant. So you'll help show me around this glorious Hall?"

Anne couldn't help but feel her cheeks turning crimson red in his company once again.

"I'll have to keep an eye on this one," Charles joked.

"Yes, you will!" he turned back to Anne's father with a stern face upon him.

An awkward silence fell in the room for what seemed to be an eternity. Then the stranger burst into an exaggerated laugh, triggering an auto response from Charles and Jane to join him.

After finishing breakfast, the tour began on the third floor, Charles' way of showing just how many rooms and space he had at his disposal and ended in The Tapestry Room.

"This is Anne's favourite room these days," Charles mocked.

"I can see why, it must have taken a lot of time and effort to present such pieces."

"We still get a lot of them as gifts and I have them displayed in here, many find them intriguing however some don't like the atmosphere in here. Maybe it's due to all the different, elaborate designs and cultures all stored in one room or something, I don't know," Charles grinned.

"Some people are just easily uneased, and once one person becomes uncomfortable, the rest either follow like sheep or the person is outcast, aren't they?" the dark stranger replied.

"I suppose so," Charles replied, not quite knowing what to make of the response he had just been given. "Anyway, please make yourself at home until you are able to continue on your journey. If you need anything feel free to ask any of the servants. I've some business to attend to now."

As the Tottenham's were leaving the room the handsome individual called to Anne.

"Could you tell me more about these pieces?"

She looked towards her father for approval.

"Well, go on my dear don't keep the man waiting," Charles said as he closed the door behind him.

Anne knew the act was back on again in front of a guest her father was trying to impress. However, she didn't mind time alone with the new guest within Loftus Hall as she wanted to dig below the surface a little further.

"Such beautiful designs," he said.

"I know, I spend hours marvelling at them almost each day."

"Do you know who created them?" he asked.

"Not all of them but I do know who did that one," Lady Anne said pointing to a huge tapestry, with interweaving shapes and lines over the fireplace. "One of my father's friends had their servants create it as a gift to the house."

"Amazing how such talent can lay in the most unlikely of hands isn't it?" he said, turning and walking towards her, those dark eyes staring right into her soul once again.

"I know, I wish I could create something as beautiful."

"Oh, I'm sure you could do anything you put your

mind to Anne," he said rubbing her cheek hypnotically with the back of his hand.

"There is nothing special about me, just a lonely woman in a big house," she said, sinking into her shoulders.

Moments later a knock came to the door. "Lunch is ready," one of the servants called out, and with that the pair left the Tapestry Room.

Over the next number of days, Anne and her new *friend* started spending more and more time together. They would share walks throughout the Hall and spend hours in the Tapestry Room enjoying their surroundings and each other's company. Anne learned he was an extremely knowledgeable man who by all accounts had seen many parts of the world and had many more yet to explore. She did ponder where he originated from due to the difficulty of pinning down his deep accent, however she didn't want to appear intrusive or rude by delving deep into his past. She was just happy to finally be able to share time with an interestingly mysterious individual who appeared to enjoy her company just as much she did his. Plus, having looks which took the young ladies breath away and made her heart quiver was a bonus.

One week after he arrived, the pair were sharing

some of their usual time together in the Tapestry Room.

"You know every time I set foot in here, I always find something new to marvel at," Anne said, taking in a deep breath of wonder and fulfilment.

"This room does indeed contain a lot of beauty, however none such as yours."

Anne felt a wave of excitement crash over her, however shyness was still getting the better of the young beautiful lady.

Turning to him she said, "I'm sure you've seen far prettier women on your travels."

"I have seen many a woman but none as beautiful and unique as you."

With that, he stepped over to her, taking her hands in his, he gently kissed her soft, sweet lips. Stopping momentarily, Anne looked into those deep, dark eyes. Smiling at her, he placed a comforting hand upon her left cheek and they embraced in a long, passionate kiss. This is what Lady Anne had yearned for, for so long. Someone to spend time with and someone to embrace and love her.

After the kiss, the pair shared a cheeky grin, before chatting some more in their own private world they could share in the flamboyant room.

Each day the couple would spend hours alone in the Tapestry Room. So much so others began to notice.

"They spend a lot of time in there don't they?" Jane said to Charles sitting down to dinner as dusk was beginning its slow decent around the Hall.

"Yes I've noticed that myself. I hear them chatting in there from time to time when I walk by."

"Let's hope that's all they are doing in there," Jane said, forking food into her mouth.

"What do you mean?" Charles shot back.

"Well come on now Charles, a handsome young man and let's face it, a beautiful woman, together, alone in a room constantly. I doubt it takes much for your imagination to put together what they could also be doing in there."

The very thought of his chaste, virginal daughter in the embrace of the dark stranger sent a rattling rage coursing through his veins. He was the only person who picked the right men for his daughters and although the new dweller did fit the bill, the man of the house had not officially given his blessing.

"You think they are really up to something together?" he said, dropping the cutlery firmly onto the table in front of him.

"Oh, I don't know for sure, but it's possible isn't it? Plus Anne had been mopping about the place before he arrived and now there seems to be a spring in her step wouldn't you say?"

"I suppose you're right. She seems to enjoy being around him. I better keep an eye on them, I am the one who decides what happens in this house," Charles stated, slashing into a piece of meat aggressively at the thought of someone getting one over on him.

Jane responded with a smile.

Later that evening, Charles stood resting against one of the large, thick staircase banisters, with a candle proudly perched upon it, waiting for the Tapestry Room doors to slowly swing open and for the cosy pair to emerge into his judgemental sight.

He gritted his teeth listening to the unaware pair softly giggle inside. The thought of storming in and throwing a piece of his mind at them shot into his mind, however as satisfying as that would have been for him, he decided against it. He concluded that if he examined their faces upon exiting the room, only then would they show their true guilt if anything indeed was going on between them.

Not long afterwards, the large wooden doors

slowly squeaked open and out stepped Anne followed by her company for the evening.

"I must get those hinges looked at shouldn't I?" Charles said, arms folded, watching his daughter's face drop to the cold floor in front of him.

She didn't respond.

"Maybe I should get them removed altogether eh?" he continued. "Yes I bet that would remove the problem," Charles' eyes turning to the deep, dark ones glaring back at him.

"Charles, how are you?" the man asked, donning the black attire he wore the night he arrived at the Hall.

"I'm wondering what you two do be getting up to in there behind my back." Charles snarled.

This triggered one of those trademark grins from the visitor. An awkward silence passed until finally the dark stranger, who seemed to be immune to Charles' intimidation, stretched out his right hand in the direction of the Tapestry Room.

"Come inside and we'll talk about it?" his grin growing ever wider and eyebrows scrunching together more firmly.

Suddenly Charles felt a feeling he had never felt before. Slowly creeping through him was a wave of anxiety and the longer he stared into those two dark abysses on the man's face, the more uncomfortable he became. Unable to put his finger on the reason for the sudden change in his mood, in his mind his authority had just been challenged and he somehow knew that if he accepted the contest, he would come out on the losing side.

"Not at all, only joking. I was wondering if you wanted to join us for a card game. I have guests coming over in a bit," Charles said, not believing the words had just passed his own lips. Never in his life had he backed down anyone, especially since he had come into possession of Loftus Hall. "We'd be delighted to have you at the table," he continued.

"Well, thank you for that kind invitation but I think I'll put my head down for the evening." Turning to the beautiful, bewildered Lady Anne beside him, he kissed her on the cheek. "Thank you for a wonderful day as always," then smiling towards Charles, he passed him, and went upstairs.

Anne couldn't believe what she just witnessed. Never had she seen someone stand up to her father without even breaking a sweat and blatantly dismissing his attempt at confrontation like it was a shrivelled leaf riding away on a gust of wind.

Charles put his experience down to the tiredness of the day and decided to let it lie.

"He's lucky I was kidding with him," he said to his daughter trying to regain the alpha position in front of her. "Now go get ready for the game and even though I was joking, you better not be up to something in there do you hear me?" He instructed, before getting ready for the card game.

As Charles got dressed, he laughed into the huge, luxurious mirror, wondering what the hell had come over him downstairs. *You're slowly losing it old boy,* he thought pulling on the fine, cream jacket with gold fastenings around his shoulders. *Just bide your time and then let him know who's the boss around here,* he instructed himself while adjusting the cuffs. Happy with his appearance, he went back downstairs to begin his night of unwinding, hopeful the whiskey may bring him back to his senses a little.

The card game and alcohol quickly reached full swing. Lightening flashed against the Hall as a thunder storm roared a few miles out to sea. Watching the flashes bounce against the curtains, Anne turned and eyed a shadow pass by the slightly ajar door leading to the main staircase. Eyes adjusting, she watched the crack of the doorway fill with a familiar profile. He stood there smiling, his teeth glistening in the candle light. He winked at her then moved away.

"Thank God that storm is staying away from the land eh?" one of the guests said picking up his cards.

"Yes I'm sure it'll ease later," Charles replied, taking a huge swig of whiskey.

"I'll be back in a second," Anne said standing from the table.

Charles rolled his eyes and continued with the game.

Closing the door behind her, she eyed the man she was slowly falling for, standing where her father had stood just hours before. Walking towards him, the lightening ricocheted off the glass roof opening, reaching him she watched it twinkle in his eyes.

"I couldn't stay away from you without getting one more kiss," he said, taking her in his arms.

Closing her eyes, he placed his lips on hers as the lightening danced around them. At that moment, Anne truly believed she was finally experiencing love, a feeling which she never wanted to lose.

Chapter 7

As the days passed, it became harder for Anne to separate herself from the man of her dreams. They spent the majority of their time together in one another's embrace. She found herself waiting for him to rise in the morning so they could have breakfast together and then stroll about the grand Hall or retire to the Tapestry Room.

Over the last number of weeks, Anne had been showered with every compliment imaginable and prayed the Atlantic waters would never become calm again. She had contemplated telling the man who randomly walked into her life on that dark stormy evening, exactly how she felt about him. However, she thought it better to wait, reasoning that stating ones love at such an early stage may force him to jump back onto his ship and brave the unforgiving waves as quickly as he possibly could. She also knew she would have to keep her love hidden from her father because he would have the final say in the whole matter.

Charles was just about hitting boiling point with the whole situation. He didn't like not knowing exactly what was going on in that room between the pair and the thought of being made a fool of in his own home didn't sit too well with him. He knew he couldn't just start throwing around wild accusations without any evidence because he would look just as much a fool. He decided to bide his time, rationalising they would soon slip up and he also knew the sea couldn't stay choppy forever.

"Dinner is ready!" Charles said, swinging open the Tapestry Room door instead of one of the servants, confident he was going to catch the pair in an embarrassing situation.

His smile lessened when he eyed Anne pointing out the finer detail on one of the tapestry works.

"You two are very cosy aren't you?" he added, folding his arms.

"Who wouldn't be, surrounded by such fine work as this? I still find it unbelievable the patience the person who created this must have had, simply remarkable." the dark stranger said.

"And you Anne, you must be bored to death in here by now. You live in this room," Charles said, casting his eyes towards her.

Anne felt the stare of interrogation weighing upon her and she glanced nervously towards the man whom she couldn't get out of her mind even if she wanted to.

"Dinner smells lovely, I'm starving," he said to Charles, before Anne had any time to respond.

"Come and get it while it's warm," the man of the house said spinning and walking back out through the door.

"After you," the charming fellow said to Anne with his arm stretched before him.

She didn't know which was the most obvious; the smile on her face or the redness which was burning along her cheeks. He was perfect in every sense of the word and she couldn't get enough of his charm.

"This looks delicious," Anne's infatuation said, sitting down at the table, after he had helped seat Anne of course.

"The sea seems to have calmed a little out there today," Charles said, looking out under his eyebrows.

"I hadn't noticed," the man returned, shoving a large piece of meat into his mouth.

"Yes maybe you'll have time for one more card game before you set sail?"

Anne couldn't believe the words she was hearing but she also knew by her father's tone that he wasn't happy and he wanted the stranger to set off on his way as soon as possible. It was obvious his welcome had well and truly reached its end.

"You know, you're right. I was going to set off once the weather had eased enough and judging by what you've informed me of, I will be able to take to the waters again tomorrow. I'd be delighted to join you for one more card game but don't blame me if you look the fool," he replied with that same dark hole in his eyes and a brazen grin etched across his chiselled face.

The same uncomfortableness began to seep through Charles once again, however he was determined not to let the subtle intimidation get the better of him.

"Ah, I don't think that will happen at all," Charles shot back at him.

"Oh, you men and your ego's," Jane said, picking up a spoon and stirring her tea.

"Not at all dear, just some friendly competition. Isn't that right friend?" Charles jousted across the table through the flickering candle light.

"Of course, but I still don't think you've got a chance after what I've seen up until now."

Charles didn't know how to react. He was being talked down to in front of his family by someone who seemed to care not about his status.

The dark stranger spouted into a burst of laughter

as he gently slapped his palm off the table. Instantly, Charles joined in assuming the whole chat had been a joke, however it still didn't change how much he wanted him gone.

"Oh you're a good one I tell you," he said, waving his finger, smirking. "Okay I'm going to go get ready. The guests will be arriving in about an hour,"

Charles stood from the table and made his way to his bedroom to get changed. Jane followed soon afterwards leaving Anne and her love alone with the servants as they cleaned up the dinner cutlery.

"So you're really going to leave then?" the natural beauty said as the tears began to trickle down her cheeks. "I should have known it was all too good to be true."

"I just have some business to take care of, but if you'll have me, I'll be back in a couple of weeks," he said turning to her.

"Really, you'd come back for me?" Anne said as he wiped away one of her glistening tears.

"Of course I would, and I will. I really like you Anne. Would you like me to come back to you?"

"Yes of course, please don't leave me alone in this place. I'll wait for you." she said.

The two, making sure they were alone, kissed

passionately as they had done so many times before in private. Anne's heart had been refilled with love, a love she would gladly wait another number of weeks to share with this man. Instead of letting the sadness of his departure get to her, the young lady decided to concentrate on the happiness she would feel once he returned.

The pair left the table and returned to their rooms to prepare for the night ahead. It was the first time for as long as Anne could remember she wasn't dreading the company and the theatrical play she was taking part in. Her mind was on other things. She was dreaming of their perfect life together once he returned and about finally getting out of her lonesome rut.

Later that evening, Charles bumped into the stranger in the corridor.

"I don't mean to be rude, but it really is time you were moving on. I sure you are a busy man and have plenty to attend to once the weather is calmer," Charles said.

"I've really gotten to like it here Charles," the stranger said.

"Listen, enough of these stupid games!" Charles, stepping forward, said through gritted teeth, "I've had enough of this crap, I don't know who you think you are, but this is my house and I don't want you here anymore, you've outstayed your welcome. So leave soon or else."

There was no response, as he stared into those cold, dark eyes which seemed to pierce straight into Charles soul.

"Have I made myself clear?" Charles continued, trying to keep the aggression flowing.

Seconds later, knocking sounded on the front door, the stranger smiled, turned and walked away from the man of the house. Opening the door, one of the many servants who were on duty for the night welcomed in Charles' guests. In through the doors once again stepped Johnathan and his wife Rosaline, the rain and wind gently patting them on their backs. Johnathan's brother Francis couldn't make it due to feeling unwell.

"I'm looking forwards to this," Rosaline said, handing her jacket to the servant.

"Me too, you know we both can't win right?" Johnathan winked.

"I'm not planning on letting you win anyway," his wife laughed back towards him.

Turning right, they once more walked into the Card Room, which as usual was decorated by the swaying flames burning on top of the various candles. The pair took their seats, facing the glorious fire. Instantly they were handed an alcoholic beverage.

Moments later, the door swung open and in walked Charles and Jane. Charles with whiskey in hand, determined to be undeterred by the response to the instructions he had just given.

"You looking forward to loosing again old boy?" he said sitting opposite his friend.

"I never lose twice in a row my friend."

"We'll see," Charles smirked.

The two ladies began to engage in some friendly chit chat while they waited for the game to begin. Not long afterwards, Anne and her friend made their way into the room and over to the large table. Anne sat beside her step mother and the dark stranger across from her. She found it a little strange she didn't know what he did for a living, however she felt when he returned they would be able to get to know each other further. He was wearing the same dark attire he worn on the first night he arrived at Loftus Hall.

Charles began to deal the first round of cards around the table, the rain outside tapping against the room's huge windows.

"How are you finding life here at Loftus?"

Johnathan asked the man sitting beside his wife, picking up his cards.

"He won't be here much longer," Charles quickly spouted across the table. "He is planning to be on his way very soon."

"It's an amazing structure. I'm glad I got to witness it," the stranger said looking down at the cards in his hands.

"You're planning to be on your way soon? I hope the weather outside isn't brewing up anything nasty," Rosaline added to the conversation.

"Ah, he'll be fine," Charles smirked.

Revealing his cards, the smirk quickly disappeared, noting the visitor to their lives had just gotten off to a winning start.

"Are you sure you really want to play this game?" he grinned towards Anne's father, sending an icy chill along his spine.

The night rolled on as storm winds began to swirl around the grounds outside as the whiskey flowed at the table like a fast running river. Charles and the dark stranger continued to throw snide remarks back and forth to one another.

"May I say Jane, you look incredibly beautiful this evening. I'd say you've broke many a heart," the man said, glaring at her with his deep, dark eyes.

"Thank you," she replied, beginning to blush, as Anne had so many times before with his charm.

"You're welcome, however I have to say Anne is the most beautiful woman here," the dark stranger said winking at her, then grinning at Charles.

"Okay enough of this crap, let's get a move on okay!" Charles said, collecting the cards off the table, getting ready to deal once more. "You going to chat nonsense all night or play cards?" he continued, a fury building inside him due to the blatant disrespect and the disregard of his authority.

"Come on now Charles, no need to get angry," he returned, smile widening.

"Just shut up and play," Charles said throwing the cards around the table once again.

Everyone, including Jane, felt uncomfortable at the table, sensing a fight would break out any moment. Flicking a card towards Anne, it slide off the table and onto the floor beneath her. Sensing her father's anger building, she quickly bent down to retrieve it as not to hold up the game and it was at that very moment she wished she hadn't.

Her eye's widened in horror as she stared across beneath the table to see in the swaying candle light, long tuffs of thick, dark hair and a cloven hoof at the end of the dark stranger's left leg. The young lady instantly let out a shriek of terror and shot back to her original seating position in shock.

"What the hell are you screaming at?" Charles snarled.

Anne just stared blankly at the stranger in front of her.

"Anne?" Charles snapped.

Anne didn't know what she had just witnessed and felt nauseated watching the stranger glaring back at her.

Suddenly, the dark stranger began to giggle loudly. This quickly burst into a loud, ear piercing, wild laughter as he continued to stare at the perplexed young Lady Anne.

Charles turned to him, as did the others, all wondering what was happening. Without any warning, the stranger slammed his hand hard onto the table and he erupted into immense flames. Turning to Charles, everyone in the room by then wincing due to the high pitch volume of the sadistic laugh and horrified by the scene unfolding in front of them. The burning *man* stood from his chair. This caused the others to quickly move away from him. The putrid smell of burning flesh filled the air and arms outstretched beside him, the stranger uttered the word "Pathetic!" and with that the flames totally engulfed him. A thunderous bang filled the room causing all within it to dive for cover and the flames shot towards the high ceiling, within seconds he was gone.

Looking upwards, Charles eyed a huge hole above where the stranger had sat. The edges of which were still glowing red from the extreme heat which had just burst through it.

"What the hell just happened?" Johnathan uttered, climbing back to his feet.

No response came. Instead, a wide mouthed Charles walked over to the opposite side of the table and gingerly leaned beneath the great crevasse and peered upwards. Instantly, a splash of rain thumped against his forehead. To his amazement, the hole had seared its way through each floor above him and out into the thick night sky.

"Who was he and how did he do that?" Johnathan continued, disbelief rattling through his mind, as too the others.

"I've no idea," Charles said swinging open the Card Room door, making his way to the main doors.

Racing out into the cold, howling damp night. Glancing up to the roof he couldn't see a glow of burning flames anywhere against the darkness. He decided to circle the building, trying to rationalise what he had just witnessed. Walking around the grand Hall, the heavy whistle of the wind and the cold rain slapping against him accompanied by the sound of the waves beating against the peninsula in the distance, were the only things which were evident. There was no burning manic prowling the grounds, no apparent fire on the roof, or no charred remains in the gardens. He had just disappeared into the night.

Charles made his way back to the main door where the others who had experienced the hideous event, were waiting for an update, each one of them holding a candle to help fight back the night.

"Anything out there?" Rosaline asked, quivering beside her husband.

"Where did he go?" Anne added.

"There's nothing out here, not one sign of him. This has to be some kind of joke or something, no one can just burst into a ball of flames and disappear like that!" Charles said, passing by them back into the Hall.

However, the reality of the situation hit him once again as he looked back up at the charred, smoking

THE LEGEND OF LOFTUS HALL

hole in the ceiling.

"Get a damn bucket or something," he roared to one of the servants watching the rain water collect on the Card Room floor.

"I think we should get going," Johnathan said, the terrifying event had sobered him up quite a bit.

"Ok, but keep this to yourselves until we get to the bottom of this!" Charles instructed with a stern glare.

Indeed the couple would keep it to themselves, because first of all they could not explain what they had just witnessed and second, who would believe them. Quickly gathering their coats, they sped out into the rain, occasionally peering back over their shoulders to ensure there was no burning lunatic casing after them.

"Where did he go?" Anne once again asked with a look of both bewilderment and terror etched across her face.

"Go to bed Anne," her father instructed. "Anne!" He said again in a raised voice watching her puzzle over what had happened.

The young lady did as instructed.

Laying down on her bed, there was no chance she was going to get any sleep even if she tried. Anne couldn't get that dreadful laughter or the sickening image of the burning man out of her mind. Another disturbing image which lingered in her mind was that of the cloven hoof she eyed beneath the table. Her head was awash with questions with impossible answers. Downstairs she could hear her father barking instructions to the workers, trying no doubt to clean up the mess and prevent his authority being questioned and to keep watch during the night hours for any sign of the dark stranger.

At dawn Anne quickly jumped from the bed, tiredness still had its grasp on her unrested body. Still donning the attire from the night before, she raced downstairs into the Card Room. She was instantly greeted with the smell of burnt flesh and timber, turning towards the ceiling she knew it hadn't all been just in her imagination. There above the card table was a large hole scorched into the structure.

Walking over to it, as Charles did the night before, she leaned over and peeked up through it. It was still raining however Charles had obviously gotten a number of workers to carry out some quick repair work, evident by the large planks and huge canvas cover stretched over the outer roof. Hearing rustling about upstairs, she knew the house would be alive with movement once again for the day, so she decided to go into the Tapestry Room and reflect on what had happened.

Closing the doors gently behind her, she made her

way over to the heavy, tall, green curtains and slid them slightly back. Staring out into the pouring rain she wondered what had happened to the man of her dreams and why he reacted in the way he did. It was all too much for her to comprehend.

Why did you leave me? Passed into her mind, *You said you'd come back for me, are you going to come back?* She couldn't believe these thoughts were bombarding her mind, clearly something unexplainable had happened right in front of her eyes, making him something not natural, however her heart still yearned for him.

"Anne you in there?" it was her father.

"Yes," she replied.

Opening the door, in walked the man of the house.

"I can't have you walking alone around the place just yet, we have to make sure he isn't still here. Come with me," he instructed.

Charles gathered dozens of his servants in the Main Hall and instructed them to search each room, hallway, cupboard, and bathroom and once the Hall was clear they were instructed to move out onto the grounds and search behind each tree, bush, flower bed, and building to establish if the dark stranger was indeed still present on the site. They were commanded to leave nothing unturned.

Hours passed as Charles, Jane, and Anne waited in the Morning Room for an update. It was late afternoon when the final word came back that each void in and around Loftus Hall had been searched, nothing out of the ordinary was found, and the ship which had been docked at the harbour nearby had also vanished.

Learning this, Charles permitted Anne to go about her daily business again, for all it was worth and instructed some of the groundskeepers to prepare and fix the ceiling in the Card Room. After all, he couldn't have guests coming over and be smacked in the face with a huge gaping hole in the ceiling. Not only would it be an eye sore, but it would also give the false indication that he didn't have the ability, or funds to have it repaired. In his opinion, it needed to be addressed as quickly as possible.

Using a mixture quickly put together, the groundskeepers managed to seal the hole after a few hours, which by then, night had firmly collapsed upon the peninsula. Aided by candle light, Charles surveyed the ceiling and was satisfied with their work.

"We'll get this painted tomorrow," he said and then dismissed them for the evening.

Charles couldn't explain what happened during the card game, however knowing the fiend had left the building was good enough for him. He didn't want to linger on such things and was determined to move on and try to forget about the whole experience.

After dinner, the family retired for the night to try to gain the sleep they had lost through a mixture of shock and fear the night before.

It didn't take Anne long to slip into a nightmare. She was running down the long avenue from Loftus Hall and the faster she ran, the less ground she seemed to cover as the building behind her appeared to grow bigger and bigger, gaining ground on her. It was then she saw him. Before her was the dark stranger standing between the two large, stone pillars at the main entrance. That grin, that unsettling but charming grin etched upon his face. She stopped dead in her tracks.

"I told you I'd come back for you," he said, and then as he did at the table, burst into a blaze of flames. He slowly walked towards her with his arms outstretched, pieces of burning clothing falling to the ground beneath him. "Come to me Anne," as a hideous laughter filled the air.

Anne shot from her slumber, drenched in sweat, and quickly glanced around the room. No one was standing in the shadows waiting to pounce on her. Realising it was a bad dream, she rested back on her mattress once again. Staring into the darkness she knew she was once more alone in that large, cold house. She had witnessed a terrifying, unexplainable event and wondered who the man she had fallen for really was, and how did he manage to do what he did in front of the card players at the table and the servants standing by in the room. All of these weighing questions bombarded her mind and soon she found her eye lids sewing themselves together again.

The following morning, Charles was the first to rise. Getting dressed, he quickly made his way downstairs and went out to the Coach House. Rounding up two servants with paint buckets, brushes and a ladder, they made their way back into the Hall. Stepping past the glorious staircase, Charles pushed open the Card Room door and was instantly greeted by darkness. Stepping passed the fireplace on his right, which still had tiny red embers twinkling within the ash, he went into the Drawing Room. He flicked back the four huge sets of curtains and walked back out passed by the old piano which very rarely emitted a sound. Charles quickly pulled back the curtains in the Card Room. As daylight flowed into the room, Charles spotted large pieces of plaster laying on the floor. Looking upwards, every single piece of material that was used to cover the hole left in the ceiling by the malicious act had fallen to the ground.

"You couldn't even do one thing right!" Charles

roared at the pair. "Clean up this damn mess and fix that ceiling before I really lose my temper," he snarled.

Bewildered as to how the filling had fallen to the floor, the petrified servants asked no questions and got straight to work.

Once the mess was cleared, the workers made an extra thick batch of plaster and once again applied it to the defiant open feature dominating the room.

Most of the morning was spent repairing and redoing the work from the previous day and during the afternoon the application was allowed to dry.

It was early evening when a coat of paint was brushed onto the ceiling. Once finished, they called for Charles.

"Let's hope it stays there this time eh? I don't like double jobbing you know!" he said inspecting the area. "One more coat of paint tomorrow and it should be fine though," Charles said arms folded. "Okay go on get out of here. I've better things to be doing than double checking your work," he said, leaving the room while the workers tidied up their equipment.

The following morning, Charles awoke bright and early and ventured into the Card Room to examine the repairs. To his disbelief, there on the floor before him again were large lumps of plaster, above which was the rebellious crevasse which was just short of laughing at his attempts to conceal it. Furious at the shoddy workmanship, Charles called the doomed workers into the Hall and spat every insult he could think of at them before unceremoniously kicking them off the estate.

Charles had others, including reputable builders, repair the hole in the Card Room ceiling countless times until he finally concluded that it was futile task. It was clear the dark stranger had left his mark on the Hall and it was there to stay. It was purposed that the hole was too large and the only way to repair it properly was to rebuild the entire ceiling, however Charles declined this recommendation because he felt in some way it may do no good. Of course he didn't reveal this to anyone, his excuse was that the card games would have to continue. In the end, Charles decided to have a heavy curtain draped in the corner of the room from the ceiling to floor to disguise the eye sore. Something of which would often be found in a heap on the floor and was rehung immediately.

Chapter 8

The weeks rolled slowly by as the individuals who witnessed the horrid events in the Card Room on that dark stormy night tried to put it all behind them.

This proved to be incredibly difficult because somehow the story had gotten out amongst the other servants on the estate about the dark stranger who shot through the roof in a ball of immense flame. Charles by that stage had snapped his temper towards many a person in the great Hall who felt unnerved when alone, however even he couldn't deny that the atmosphere had changed in Loftus Hall ever since that card game. It was as though there was a set of eyes on you no matter where you went in the house. Most of the rooms seemed to grow darker earlier than they should in the evening and the smell of burning flesh would mysteriously descend into the Card Room and dissipate just as quickly as it was sensed.

Charles however, put this down to the shock of the event and the paranoia spreading amongst the servants and he was convinced this would all pass in time.

Young lady Anne however, had become totally engulfed with sorrow and loneliness. Walking through the Hall, she would often see shadows moving about in the corner of her eye, turning, convinced it would be the dark stranger who had returned for her, she would be further saddened to find no one there. Her mind replayed the times they shared together over and over again. She yearned for her love to return, she longed to be with him. By then Anne would spend the majority of her waking hours in the Tapestry Room, standing between the heavy green curtains at the large middle window, staring out into the distance waiting for any sign of her beloved's return.

She only spoke to Charles and Jane when necessary and often when a groundskeeper would pass by the window she permanently frequented, he or she would wave and her response would be a gentle smile. However Anne's eyes would never move from the horizon. The beautiful young lady was heartbroken and didn't care for anything else only to see *him* again. Anne caught sight of the large curtain being rehung to cover the gaping hole in the ceiling once or twice and wondered how he could have pulled off such an act. But the loneliness in her heart was the thing bombarding her the most. When she learned the ship had vanished, she assumed he had taken it to his destination and hoped he was a man of his word and return for her.

"Dinner, now!" came rattling through the Tapestry

Room door, as Charles walked by, towards the dinner table.

He rarely called her for dinner, usually the servants had that task, however she knew when he did it was better to oblige rather than face him stamping his authority over her.

"Growing very pale aren't we," Jane said with a smirk, forking a mouthful of food into her mouth as she watched Anne sit down at the table.

There was no response.

"Don't be so rude. Do you hear me!" Charles snapped.

A servant came over to dish up a spoon full of potatoes, to which Anne raised a firm hand to signal she didn't want any.

"What's the matter, the food not good enough for you?" came the snide remark from her father.

"I'm not hungry."

"I suppose that makes sense, you do nothing all day but stare out that window."

"Just leave me alone. I'm not hurting anyone am I?" The young lady replied, feeling the tears building in her lower eye lids.

"Listen, you need to grow the hell up. Staring out a damn window for lover boy to come back to you. Well I've got news for you, he better not come back here if he knows what's good for him," Charles howled across the table. "Pulls a cheap parlour trick that almost burnt the house down. If I see him again I'll have him hung out to dry!" He said, confirming his statement by pointing his index finger hard against the table.

Anne shot up from her chair and raced away into the dark corridor.

"Let her run and hide away in a room, it's all she seems to be good for these days," Jane said, sipping on a drink.

"Oh, don't worry, I'm not running after her. She'll eat when she's starving and then she'll be thankful for what she has here."

Anne ran upstairs to her bedroom and closed the door behind her. She walked to her bed and collapsed in a torrent of tears. She felt doomed, with no prospects and with no hope of happiness in her life. Anne cried into her pillow for several hours until the fatigue of sorrow overcame her, and she drifted off to sleep.

She awoke in the early hours of the morning trembling with the cold on top of the bed. She began to pull the blankets over herself when the word,

"Anne..." slowly floated through the darkness.

Raising her tired body to her elbows, she looked towards the door which was by then open. Aided by the bright moonlight and cloudless sky outside, she eyed a familiar silhouette standing within the door frame. Without warning it turned and walked away from her. In disbelief, she hopped from the bed and made her way to the door. Turning, she saw *him* walk towards the main staircase. Not wanting to wake anyone, she kept her lips sealed and followed him. The Hall always looked eerie to her during the night hours and that night was no different. She couldn't believe she was following this man through the darkness.

Walking down the stairs, Anne spotted a flickering light emanating from behind the Card Room door which was partially closed.

Her heart was racing so rapidly she thought it was going to burst through her chest. The young lady placed the palm of her hand gently upon the door, took a deep breath, and slowly pushed it open. When she saw who was inside, her jaw hit the floor. Sitting in the same seat he was on the night before he left Loftus Hall was her beloved dark stranger.

"Anne," he said. "Come join me," pointing to the

chair pulled out from the table opposite him.

Stunned beyond all belief, she moved her legs in the direction of the table.

"You must be wondering why I'm here like this?" he said with that trademark smirk on his face, "I told you I'd come back for you."

"How...how did you do that?" Anne said pointing to the roof. "Who are you?"

"Anne my dear you don't need to fear me, I'm here for you. However, you should be worried about your father." He said, dismissing her question as he clasped his hands on the table.

"My father?" she said, confusion slowly seeping into her more.

"He isn't all he's built himself up to be you know."

"What do you mean?"

"I know things about him Anne, upsetting things."

"Do I really want to hear this?" the young lady said shuffling uneasily in the chair.

"He has lied all his life Anne, he's always lied to you and your sister." Leaning forward slightly he continued, "He never really loved your mother you know. He only married her for the title and power which came with the marriage. In fact, Anne Loftus had loved another other than him. He knew this however and had the man threatened to stay away from her and if he didn't, well I'm sure to can guess the ultimatum. And who knows what he may have done to finally marry her, maybe he did have him killed."

Anne couldn't believe what she was hearing and the stranger sensed her mistrust,

"Come on, is it really that hard to believe what I've just told you after all you've witnessed over the years? He only cares about his own happiness and title, no one else matters to him. You and your sister are the heirs to the Loftus estate and if word of his devious acts to marry into the family and what he may have done to achieve it were to get out, well that would truly be retribution for your poor mother's unhappiness wouldn't it?" he grinned.

"But how do you know all of this?"

"I know many things Anne. I know how much you loved your mother, I know how much you love your sister, I know how lonely you are in this place, and I know deep down you believe me."

It was true, the words she had just heard made sense and if they indeed were true then her father was a truly terrible man, however she would need to find out for sure.

"I've to go now Anne, but I'll be back for you," he said, rising from the table,

"Go? Why must you leave?" she said, still not fully coming to terms with what she had awoken to.

"I'll be back to you Anne."

He walked from the Card Room and returned to the main door. Opening it he vanished into the darkness before she could ask another question.

The next morning Anne awoke feeling extremely dizzy, with a misty haze coating her vision. Rubbing her eyes, she noted that her bedroom door was closed. Stepping from her bed she went downstairs to the Card Room where she and the stranger had spoken the night before. Walking inside, she could see the candle on the table was as fresh as the day it was placed there not long ago. There was no indication it had been used as she remembered when she ventured down the glorious staircase hours before and following its light onto the room.

Was it just a dream? Her head began to ache. All logic leading to the answer to her question was yes, because Loftus Hall was a place you just couldn't walk into at night without being noticed. She knew she surely would have asked him more questions if he had visited her the night before. Yawning, she rationalised that it was indeed a dream, however a seed of doubt was still in her mind. There was also the unsettling revelation about her father which was disclosed to her by the dark stranger.

What if her mother truly loved someone else and Charles had that individual *disposed* of, surely, he couldn't live with himself after that she thought. However, Anne was determined to quiz her father about it because she couldn't bear to live with someone who did that to her mother. Her mind wouldn't rest unless she knew the truth.

"Anne, lunch!" She was in the Tapestry Room and the sound of her father's voice sent a quiver rattling through her bones.

She was standing in her usual spot at the window, having spent the last number of hours wondering if she had or had not spoken to her beloved within her slumber during the night.

"Anne!" a voice roared louder outside and the doors were flung open.

In walked a high tempered Charles. "I'm getting sick of this you know. I've more things on my mind than looking after a foolish child,"

"What, like why you married mother?" she

couldn't believe the words fell from her mouth.

"What?" Charles snarled.

"Did you love her?" Anne asked turning to him.

"What kind of stupid question is that, of course I did! Now stop this foolishness and go get your lunch,"

"She didn't love you though did she?" From somewhere Anne had finally found the courage to stand up for herself.

"How dare you speak about us like that," the irate man said stepping closer. "Keep up this nonsense and you'll be sorry."

"What like the man she had really fallen for?" Every muscle in Anne's body was rattling, she didn't know if it was from fear or anger.

Charles' face suddenly changed as though he had been punched in the stomach. "What did you just say?"

"Did you marry her just for this place?"

"You're talking pure nonsense you know that. You're spending too much time in this room, it's turning you insane."

"You did didn't you? You married her because you

just wanted the riches and title that came with the Loftus family. You knew my mother loved someone else and you forced her to marry you! What did you do with him, did you have him killed?" Anne could feel herself being overwhelmed by a wave of emotion.

Charles stood looking at her briefly.

"I can see by your reaction it must be true. Well, I'm going to tell everyone about this. I'm leaving to stay with Elizabeth today," Anne continued, quickly walking towards the door.

Passing him, Charles suddenly latched onto her right arm.

"Where do you think you're going? You think you can spout that at me and get away with it?" he said tossing her back into the room.

"What the hell are you doing?" his daughter said, racing to the door once again.

Charles however caught her and flung her hard to the ground.

"I can't have you going around spreading poison about me. I hope you really like it in here because this is where you're going to stay until you learn some damn manners," he said, turning, slamming, and locking the doors behind him.

Several servants where passing by as he locked his

daughter into the Tapestry Room. She was pounding her fists against the solid doors screaming as they glanced towards him. He shot a look towards the group, a look which deterred them from even thinking about questioning the situation.

Later that evening, Charles was back outside the Tapestry Room doors with a number of helpers. He instructed them not to pay any attention to the frantic woman inside, and that was enough, he didn't need to explain himself any further to them. Telling one of the men to remain at the door so she couldn't escape, the others collected the old, steel framed single bed, double green and white doored wardrobe and clothing rack. Unlocking the doors, Anne darted towards freedom. Two of the servants restrained her quickly as the others made their way inside with the simple pieces of furniture.

Charles instructed them to place the rickety bed in front of the middle window at the far side of the room, with the wardrobe placed at the right-hand side of the room, and the clothing rack to the left.

"Please don't do this," the young lady pleaded.

"You need to get better Anne, and this is the only way," her father said with a sneer on his face. "You've spent so many hours in here, I thought it to be the best place for you to stay for a while." He walked towards one of the beautiful tapestries decorating the wall and unceremoniously pulled it to the floor. "Can't have any distractions either. Tear them all down!" he said to the servants who got to work at once.

Watching her father's enjoyment as they removed the items she had admired for so long, made her feel sick to the core. She couldn't believe he had done this to her so to conceal what she believed to be a dark secret he was hiding from everyone.

Surely someone will question all of this! She thought watching the last of the fine handworks hit the floor. The only decoration left in the room was the bland, striped wallpaper, which was torn in places after the removal process. Charles then closed the large window shutters and locked them into position. Instantly, a thick darkness engulfed the room.

"Can't have you breaking windows and hurting yourself can we?" Charles mocked.

Gathering all the tapestries, the workmen left the room to Charles and Anne.

"Why are you doing this to me?" she sobbed.

"No one threatens me, not even my own!" Charles stated.

"You can't keep me locked away in here."

"Oh we'll see about that. As far as I'm or anyone

else is concerned now, you've lost your mind and we are doing everything we can to comfort you. Good luck trying to convenience anyone otherwise!" her father snarled.

Moments later, one of the men returned with a candle stick holder with numerous candles lighting upon it. He sat it on top of the fireplace and left. Charles smiled at his daughter and then slammed the doors behind him.

Hearing the lock turn in the doors, the distraught woman was left alone with her thoughts. Glancing around the room at what she could see of the bare walls beneath the wallpaper, they looked like a terrible decorator's attempt to cover them, Anne prayed she would awake from her nightmare at any moment. However, she knew deep down it was real and who would believe her now over her father's words. This was the beginning of a cunning ploy to give people the illusion that she had gone mad.

Turning, she collected the candles and walked over to the shutters. She already knew she could not pry them open however she tried once or twice at each one with no luck.

Surrendering to the fact she was trapped, she ventured over to the bed. She placed the candles a safe distance away from the thin linen and sat down onto the bed.

Sobbing into her hands, she thought of her mother and what she must have gone through with such a man. Anne thought of her sister, who would surely help her out of the dreadful situation if she knew about it. Finally, her mind turned to the mysterious man who had informed her of her father's cruel intentions for marrying her mother. She wondered how he would have known such things, which judging by her father's actions, were true. More to the point, she wondered, as many times before, who was this man?

The young woman lay on the bed and after hours of crying, drifted off to a broken sleep.

Later that evening, Charles prepared to get into bed. Jane as always had got there before him.

"How long are you going to leave her in there?" Jane asked her husband who was buttoning up his night wear.

"As long as it takes, she needs to learn her lesson!" he said, climbing in beside her.

"Won't the guests ask questions?" she returned.

"Who cares what anyone asks. I'm the boss in this house and as far as anyone is concerned, she has lost her mind and we are doing our best for her," he snapped.

"Okay, I'm only asking in case someone wonders about her that's all."

"If anyone wants to ask questions, tell them to ask me about her. I won't be long putting them straight. What we do in our house is our own business."

"I know dear. I totally agree with you," Jane said, reaching across and kissing him on the cheek, before turning to go to sleep.

Chapter 9

As time rolled by, Anne slowly slipped into a dark abyss within her mind. She no longer had any contact with anyone other than those who brought food and fresh clothing to her. When the servants opened the doors, they would often be greeted by her sitting beneath a window, knees to forehead, and arms clasped tightly around her legs, talking to herself. Lack of sunlight, exercise, and controlled interaction with others was taking a great toll on her delicate body, but she still had her incredible beauty.

Many who visited the house for the first number of weeks would question where young Lady Anne Tottenham was and once they were fed the, *She's not well and getting some rest,* story repeatedly, they slowly began to stop asking for her until eventually no one asked how she was doing at all. Anne was becoming nothing more than a memory outside the Tapestry Room walls.

Charles had delegated the duties to tending to his daughter to specific individuals. They were instructed not to interact with her more than absolutely necessary and to keep the details of what they were doing and why she was in there to themselves. If they did not, he warned they would face a fate worse than hers.

Various rumours were circulating around the grand estate amongst the servants about Anne, however not one of them dared to speak it aloud. The day to day running of the Loftus Hall estate went on as usual while the young lady continued to deteriorate within the dark, cold room.

"Anne, get up!" shot a voice followed by the clink of the lock early one Sunday morning.

The daylight cut through the room and in walked Charles.

"Come on now, stop feeling sorry for yourself," he said walking over to find her in her usual position beneath the window. "Your sister is visiting today and I'm sure she'll want to see you too, so make yourself presentable and enough of this self-pity!"

No response came from his daughter, she kept head buried between her knees, with her dark hair flowing down either side on them.

Moments later, more people entered the room carrying a bowl of water, towels, shoes, and a beautiful dress.

"Get her ready," Charles barked before leaving the room.

The women did as instructed and prepared Anne for her sister's arrival later that day.

Outside, the day roared a glorious warmth as the sun shot its bright light across the peninsula. The sea was like glass as the birds playfully swooped and chirped above it. In the distance, the large gates to the estate were being pulled open, as Elizabeth arrived.

Making her way down the avenue, she took in deep inhales of the fresh sea air. It was one of those things which she could never forget about living on the peninsula, no matter how long it would have been between her visits, it always revitalised her. Turning towards the main door, the defiant eagles standing above it, she wondered as many times before how they fought off the furious winds which swept the land. She then eyed the Tapestry Room windows, shutters firmly locked in the closed position.

The letter she had received from her father seemed to be true. He had informed her Anne wasn't coping very well with their mother's death and seemed to be slowly getting worse. Charles continued by saying she had lashed out many times and he was concerned for her mental health. He made the decision she needed special care to prevent her from harming herself or others.

"Great to see you sweetheart," Charles said, kissing his daughter on the cheek. "I was beginning to think you'd forgotten where we live," he grinned.

"I was just seeing if you were too busy to miss me," she returned laughing.

"Come on, let's make the most of this weather." Charles smiled.

The pair walked about the glorious gardens for quite some time asking each other the stereotypical questions people ask when they haven't seen the other for some time. It didn't take long for the subject to change to Anne.

"So how is she," Elizabeth asked, her hands clasped in front of her.

"She isn't doing too well. She's not the same Anne she used to be at the moment I'm afraid,"

"What happened?"

"I really don't know. I think your mother's death caught up with her, that and not willing to interact with anyone can play havoc on the mind," Charles explained.

Of course, he couldn't tell her the real reason why he locked her sister away, because it would be the beginning of the end. He preferred to feed Elizabeth lies and make Anne out to be insane. Any excuse to keep the spotlight off him. Another detail he didn't disclose to his visiting daughter was that of the dark stranger. In Charles's opinion, the least amount of people who knew about him and the card game, the better.

"I suppose," she said, still baffled by the whole situation. "Can I see her?"

"Of course, you can, I told her you were coming to visit. Just be warned, she may be a little delirious and might not make much sense. We had to close the shutters on the windows for fear of her climbing out and disappearing. I just hope it's a phase and hopefully she will snap out of it," Charles said with as much fake compassion as he could harvest.

Stepping into the Hall, Elizabeth was greeted by numerous hellos and smiles from the busy housekeepers inside.

"I see not much has changed around here."

"Still as busy as ever," he grinned.

"Elizabeth how are you?" Said a voice from the middle floor.

Turning, she spotted Jane descending the main staircase.

"I'm doing great thanks and you?"

"No use in complaining," she grinned, "You going in to see Anne?"

"Yes I need to see how she's doing."

"I assume Charles told you everything?" Jane returned, placing a hand on her husband's shoulder.

"He did."

"That's good," she said, and stepped away to leave the pair alone outside the room.

"Here you go dear and be sure to lock it afterwards. I'll have a servant stand by to make sure everything is okay," Charles said handing her the large key. "Before you go in, we took down all the tapestries to have them cleaned and we've put some furniture in there to make her more comfortable."

Elizabeth nodded taking the key.

Unlocking the doors, she stepped inside and was instantly hit with the smell of burning candles. The room was surprisingly dark as the numerous flames flickered about on the candle stick holder in the distance. She eyed the tiny bed, wardrobe, and clothes rack, then her attention turned to the rocking silhouette behind the bed.

Casting her eyes around the room, Elizabeth spotted the bland, abandoned spaces where the beautiful art works had been removed from and the worn wallpaper they had been concealing. However, it was the whispering which drew her attention back to Anne.

"Nobody wants me, nobody wants me, nobody wants me," Anne repeated as she rocked slowly back and forth.

Looking at her sister, who hadn't lifted her head, the sight sent a feeling of discomfort through Elizabeth's body.

"Anne?" she said softly, still in disbelief it was indeed her sister in front of her.

There was no change in Anne's actions.

"Anne, it's Elizabeth,"

The rocking stopped.

"I've come to see how you're doing," Elizabeth felt stupid saying this because it was clear to her she wasn't doing well at all.

"Elizabeth?" A hoarse voice said from behind the locks of dark hair.

"Yes it's me," she smiled.

Anne raised her head to reveal a tear ridden face, which instantly erupted with joyous emotion.

"Is it really you, really? I haven't been out of here much and I don't know what's in my imagination anymore."

"It's me, I promise," Elizabeth said, stepping around the tiny bed frame, closer to her sister.

Anne slowly stretched out her arms to her. Sitting, rocking in one position for extended periods of time had made her very stiff and her joints and muscles where aching due to not getting any exercise. Anne had greatly deteriorated which was evident by the shock on Elizabeth's face seeing her sister in such a state.

"You'll have to help me." she said to her shaken sister.

Elizabeth did as she was asked and helped her sibling to her feet. The pain etched on Anne's face and the crackling of the joints demonstrated the amount of anguish the young woman was suffering.

Wrapping her arm over her shoulder, Elizabeth began to walk about the room to help Anne loosen up.

"You have to get me out of here, please, get me out of here now," she said with a sad quiver in her voice.

"I can't," Elizabeth said. "You're not well and you need to start looking after yourself."

"Oh don't fall for his tricks. He is lying, you know that right? He wants to keep me locked in here so his secret is safe," Anne returned.

"Secret?"

"Yes a dirty secret he doesn't want anyone to find out about!" Anne said as she started randomly looking about the room. Hours alone in the Tapestry Room were really weighing heavily on her mind.

"What secret?" her sister asked, eye brows scrunching closely with confusion.

"He-"

"Everything alright in here?" Charles asked sticking his head inside to ensure Anne wasn't spouting information she shouldn't be.

"Everything is fine father," Elizabeth replied.

"Well at least you got her up off the floor, none of the housekeepers could manage that. Anyway, I'll leave you to it," Charles said, shooting a warning look to Anne before closing the door behind him.

"You were saying?" Elizabeth said, trying to restart the conversation which had just been perfectly interrupted.

Anne, knowing Charles was close by, decided to keep quiet on the real reason she believed their father married their mother. "Nothing, but please can I come and stay with you for a while? I swear I'll be no trouble, you won't even know I'm there. Plus, it will help us spend more time together," she pleaded, hoping that when they were truly alone, she could tell her sister everything.

"Anne, there is nothing I want more but you need to get better first. You and I both know father won't let you beyond the walls of Loftus in this condition."

"Please, you can't leave me in here, I'm losing my mind, there's nothing wrong with me! Please just let me come home with you, please!"

Elizabeth's eyes began to swell with emotion. She would have loved Anne to stay with her for a while, but she knew she wouldn't be able to take care of her sister in such a condition.

"Anne, I can't, I'm sorry. There's nothing I can do,"

Anne's heart sank faster than a broken ship which was ploughing towards the seabed. She knew their father had wormed his way inside Elizabeth's head and she knew she couldn't blame her for believing him. *Who wouldn't?* She thought *He is a master at deceiving people and I look and sound like I'm insane.* Charles had played the perfect hand. No one would believe Anne over him, she knew that fact once she was unable to convince her sister otherwise.

"Okay, I understand," Anne surrendered.

"Look, get yourself fit and healthy again and you can come stay with me as long as you want okay?" Elizabeth said, placing a reassuring hand upon Anne's shoulder.

"Okay," Anne replied, not knowing if that day would ever come if her father had anything to do with it. By then, no amount of pleading would help her and she concluded that even if she did manage to convince her sister to take her in, there would be no chance Charles would let her off the property.

"Will you still come visit me?" she continued, resorting to the idea if she showed her sister improvements in her health she may be able to force Charles to allow her stay with her.

"Of course I will," she smiled. "You'll never get rid of me,"

The pair spent a number of hours together talking and walking about the room before Elizabeth left to go put her head down for the night. Before going upstairs, Charles, holding a candle, met her in the corridor and called to her.

"How did you find her," he said, reaching her at the foot of the stairs.

"She doesn't seem to be doing too well at all and she is totally convinced there is nothing wrong with her," she replied as they began their ascent together.

"I know, it's absolutely terrible what she is going through. I just hope it all passes soon so we can get back to normal around here," Charles said.

"Did you get any help for her?" Elizabeth said, turning to him, "surely someone could examine her."

"Oh yes, don't worry. Once I knew her illness wasn't improving we decided to take action. I contacted the doctor myself but he has unfortunately fallen ill. Once he is feeling better, he said he will be straight around to us," her father said, "He said we are doing all we can at the moment and he will decide what to do when he gets here," Charles added, finishing off the spindle of lies he had just fed her.

"I'm glad to hear that, maybe it's what she needs, just to talk to someone," Elizabeth sighed.

After giving her father a kiss on the cheek, she retired to her bedroom, not quizzing his reasoning behind Anne's slow decent into insanity. She didn't have any cause to question her father's authority. He had spun the perfect yarn and after seeing Anne in the condition she was in, the only logic was to believe him.

Watching the door close and hearing the latch locking into position, a sinister grin etched its way across the cruel man's face. As the flickering light bounced across his features, he looked as demented as the dark stranger did on the night he took his leave from the Hall. He knew no one would ever go against him and once he gave the impression he was greatly concerned about Anne, no one would have any reason to ponder otherwise.

Elizabeth remained at Loftus Hall for a week. Charles cancelled all business meetings so he and Jane could do their utmost to occupy Elizabeth's time to keep her from interacting with Anne as much as possible. However, they couldn't keep her away from her sister forever. She would stop into see her sister every evening before going to bed.

Each evening, she stepped through the Tapestry Room doors, she would find Anne in the exact same position as the last; face between her knees and arms clasped round them. During each visit, she would have to reintroduce herself and each evening Anne ended by pleading with Elizabeth to take her from the room which seemed to have weaved its cold, depressing darkness into her soul.

On the evening before her departure home, Elizabeth spent quite some time talking to her sister. It was almost as though she was lost in her own mind, however when Elizabeth interacted with her, Anne would slowly come back to the *real* world.

"Listen, I'm leaving tomorrow," Elizabeth said, stooping down and wrapping her arm around her sister.

She hadn't lifted Anne to her feet during that visit because her joints were especially sore that evening.

"Really, do you have to go? Please don't," Anne cried, to her concerned sister.

"Don't you worry, I'll be back very soon," she smiled, fighting hard to contain the tears that wanted to burst down her face.

"Promise?"

"I promise."

"You really don't know what it's like here, I want to be with you. Please don't forget about me," Anne begged, eyebrows raised, lips curling downwards.

"How could I ever do that? You're my sister, I'll always do my best for you."

A tiny smile and a single tear trickling down a cold, pale cheek was the reaction.

Elizabeth leaned across and wiped away the tear with her thumb, "Get better soon," she smiled, rising to her feet.

"Just don't forget me," Anne said, reaching for her

hand.

"Never," Elizabeth said, rubbing Anne's hand gently, as she turned and walked away, trying her utmost not to break down in front of her sister.

Watching the door close firmly back into position, loneliness once again consumed her. Anne pondered if indeed she was insane. The last number of weeks had been so sporadic, it was hard for her to determine what was real and what originated from deep within her head. She had learned being left alone with your thoughts, can be a very daunting experience and once the mind wandered, it was hard to reel it back to shore. However, seeing her sister again had lifted her spirits a little and she was determined to get out of the walls imprisoning her.

Elizabeth left the following day not knowing the evening before would be the last time she would see her sister alive.

Watching Elizabeth pass through the gates, Charles felt a huge sense of achievement wash over him. *If she couldn't convince her, she'll never convince anyone,* he thought, throwing Elizabeth a final wave as she disappeared out of sight.

"That went well, didn't it?" Jane said, smirking to him.

"It went a lot better than I thought it would."

"Come on, lunch will be ready soon, and we don't want it to be cold now do we," she said, turning back into the house.

"If it is, they'll be sorry," Charles said, confirming there was no one immune to his harshness.

Chapter 10

Anne's health slowly sank from bad to worse. She was pushing no food past her lips and was slowly withering away to nothing. She had taken up a permanent sitting position beneath the Tapestry Room windows on the cold floor. Anytime a servant would venture into the room, they would find her sobbing into her knees, arms holding them together. Even outside the doors, her haunting weeping could be heard. Charles continued to force the servants inside to collect the cold, uneaten food and offer her the usual bland meals with no reaction from Anne.

They expressed their fears to the Anne's father, however he let the concerns and his daughter fade away. To Charles, she was slowly becoming a distant memory. So much so, that when he would have guests over, he would never talk about the woman whom he had locked up against her will. Anne was a broken soul, who had been cruelly subjected to a heinous plot to keep her mouth shut and even if she didn't, her words would fall on deaf ears.

Sitting in one positon endlessly waiting for the dark stranger to come and rescue her, Anne's joints slowly began to fuse themselves in place. Even if she wanted to rise to her feet, she would not have been able to, she was permanently trapped in a sitting fetal position. She was dying.

Growing discomfort began to sweep over the housekeepers anytime they entered the Tapestry Room. The thought of being greeted by a shrivelling woman sitting within the flickering candlelight, crying continuously, who seemed to want nothing to do with this world anymore, did not set a welcoming tone.

"She's dying, isn't she," Jane said to Charles, as she turned to him on the bed.

"So I hear. That's her own problem for not eating. We can't force the food down her throat," he said unsympathetically, as he unlaced his boots.

Jane never really had any love for Anne, so her thoughts on the situation were no more in depth than the young lady's father.

"What will we tell people?" Jane asked.

"I'm not worried to be honest, it's her own doing. Sooner the better she's gone so we can be rid of her once and for all," Charles said.

Turning to find a comfortable sleeping position, he knew once she was dead, she wouldn't be able to rip the power and fortune away from him. Furthermore, he didn't need to lay a finger on Anne to get rid of her, she was doing it all herself and he was satisfied it would all be over soon.

"Lady Anne?" one of the servants called out, stepping over to her, noticing her continued sobs had silenced.

He knew from many years serving at Loftus Hall she preferred to be called Anne, however old habits die hard.

The last burning candle at her side was about to extinguish, the others smouldering.

There was no response.

"Anne?" he called again, reaching a hand out to her once flowing hair.

Again, no recognition that he was there.

Touching the top of her head, a chilling coldness ran through his fingertips. Placing the tiny plate of lunch on the floor behind him, he raised her freezing forehead to reveal a pained, pale face with lifeless eyes, which stared into the distance. Shocked at the sight, he fell backwards.

"Help!" he roared, as he watched Anne's head fall back into its original position.

Moments later, Charles was in the room.

"She's... She's..."

He didn't need to elaborate any further, Charles knew exactly what he meant and directed him to leave the room.

Watching him disappear from sight, Charles turned back to his daughter.

"You see I always win in the end," he said, walking closer to the dead woman in front of him. "Now no one will ever have to listen to your whining again and I can feed them any story I want. If you had respected me like you should have, you wouldn't have ended up in a ball of mess like this."

Upon hearing others making their way to the room, Charles kneeled beside her and placed a hand on her head.

"Give us some time!" he bellowed, demonstrating a deceptive concern for his cold, lifeless daughter.

Once alone again, he turned back to her, "You see, everyone does what they're told around here or else." He smiled as the final candle burnt to an end beside him.

Due to her fused joints and posture, a custom-made coffin had to be quickly created to hold Lady Anne Tottenham's body. When the coffin arrived at Loftus Hall, it took only one person to lift her malnourished body and place it into the casket. Charles had her placed within the box in the same seating position in which she died. She had passed away wearing a light, white dress with blue running through its front, and she had to be buried in the same garment as it was impossible to move her joints to remove it from her contorted, feeble frame.

Learning of her sister's demise, Elizabeth, in a state of disbelief, raced to the Hall. By the time she reached the Loftus estate, the lid had firmly been closed over her sister's corpse. She pleaded with her father to see her sister one last time, but he would not allow it, saying it was an unpleasant sight and it was best she remembered her as she was before she died.

"What happened to her?" Elizabeth quizzed.

"She just stopped eating, and no matter what we did we couldn't convince her otherwise," Charles explained.

"What could had driven her to this, it just doesn't make sense," the tears beginning to saturate the floor beneath her.

Charles took her in his arms, "I know, I don't know what to say. I can't believe I've lost one on my girls," he said, trying to conceal his cold hatred for Anne as much as possible.

Lady Anne Tottenham's funeral mass was celebrated in the nearby village, Fethard on Sea. Hundreds of people came to pay their respects and show their support to her sister, stepmother and cunning father.

She was laid to rest in a tomb at the church side and after the last person told her how sorry they were for her loss, Elizabeth spent time with her sister.

"I'm so sorry this had to happen to you. I should have never let it get to this. I should have taken you into my care, please forgive me Anne." she cried, staring blankly at her sister's place of rest.

"I really have no idea what you must have gone through and I'll never forgive myself for not being there for you. I hope you're at peace. I love you Anne and I'll never forget you," she said, as she left the church grounds.

Elizabeth told her father she would be returning home right away after the Mass because she couldn't face setting foot into Loftus Hall so soon after the death of another loved one. Understanding, Charles kissed her goodbye and he and Jane made their way back to the Hall.

Charles instructed that all of Anne's items were to remain in the Tapestry Room and the doors to be locked, with him having the only key to access the area where the poor lady died. He outlined to all the staff he wanted life to go on as normal, that it had been a terrible tragedy and Anne should be allowed to rest in peace.

Blowing out the last of the ground floor candles that night, Charles made his way to the ones dancing on the main staircase. Glancing towards the doors behind which he had held his daughter captive, a tiny sliver of guilt strolled into his mind, however he quickly dismissed it, rationalising she deserved everything that had happened to her and if she had obeyed him, none of it would have occurred.

Drawing in his breath in front of the flame, a slight moan caught his attention. Darting up straight, he listened. Moments later, a low guttural moan seemed to drift around him again. Confused, he stepped away and made his way over to the two large doors behind which the doomed daughter had been locked. Pressing his ear against the cold timber, he listened carefully.

About a minute passed and with it came, "You're getting jumpy in your old age Charles," he said, grinning.

Upon hearing nothing further, he ventured back to the candles on the staircase and blew each one out, laughing to himself about letting the darkness play tricks on his mind. Closing the bedroom doors for the night, silence fell across the Hall.

Charles had once again won and now that Anne was dead, he could rest easy knowing that the Loftus estate was back in his firm control.

Chapter 11

It didn't take long after Anne's death for the atmosphere to change in Loftus Hall. Many said they could hear strange moaning and sounds of the furniture moving about behind the locked doors, however Charles would have none of it, telling anyone who mentioned the eeriness that was associated with the Tapestry Room to stop their nonsense.

Lightening cracked the sky as thunder applauded its splendid demonstration of power. The winter nights had begun to roll in around Loftus Hall. Charles was spending the reminder of the evening by the warm fireplace in the Card Room reading. He had returned from a day's business, kissed Jane before she went to bed and decided to relax while taking in the harsh weather building outside.

Turning the page, he took another sip of his whiskey when something caught his attention. A scratching sound in the distance. Standing to his feet, he went into the Drawing Room, assuming one of the windows had been left ajar and the breeze was moving the curtains. But nothing. Everything was still except for the quivering candle flame upon the mantelpiece, the strange sound was originating from somewhere else.

Opening the Card Room door, he waited momentarily in the doorway. The sound came again and to his disbelief, it seemed to be coming from within the Tapestry Room. He quickly stepped over to the large doors and pressed his ear to them. Once more, the starching noise came from behind the doors. Thoughts shot through his mind of the recent stories people had told him, however he quickly brushed them aside. Fetching a candle, he returned to the door and reached into the pocket on his fine jacket. Pulling out the key, he turned the lock, flung open the door, and was greeted by dead silence.

Stepping inside, the coldness instantly wrapped its hands around him. Glancing towards the abandoned fireplace, he reasoned it was why the room was freezing. Lighting the candles beside him, he continued his search for the elusive sound.

Reaching the foot of the bed behind which Anne had died, he paused. He somehow felt as though he was being watched and had an urge to look over his shoulder. Losing the mental battle, he glanced behind him and immediately kicked himself for doing so. *If anyone saw you,* he thought to himself, thinking of his pride. Rounding the tiny bed frame, he rationalised that anyone alone in a large dark room like this would feel a little uneasy. Smiling, he thought of the loneliness Anne must have felt being in the room for so long.

Reaching out, he slowly pulled open the wardrobe door, preparing for a rat to run for its life out under his legs. Opening the door, nothing out of the ordinary was uncovered. Scratching his head trying to figure out what was going on, the Tapestry Room door suddenly slammed shut with a loud thud behind him, causing Charles to almost die of a heart attack right there on the spot.

He raced over and reopened the door, putting the event down to a draft, and wedged it into position. Turning back to the bed, his mouth almost hit the floor beneath him. Standing behind the bed, hands firmly clasped upon the steel frame was Anne Tottenham, dressed in the exact same dress she had died and been buried in. She didn't look as malnourished as she did when she met her shocking end, and her beauty had returned, however she was donning a smile which sent a shiver straight through him.

Charles quickly rubbed his eyes and to his relief she was gone. Again, he put the whole thing down to trickery of the mind.

"This place has been locked up too long," he said, stomping his way back into the room.

Setting his candle safely onto the floor beside him, he unlocked the large window shutters and fixed them all back into the open position.

"Time to let a bit of light back into this place."

He turned and caught sight of his dead daughter's clothes beside him on the clothing rack. Not a shred of regret passed through him for what he had done to her. He was thankful it all passed without a major hitch and now the annoyance in his life could fade away into the past.

Leaving the room, Charles once again locked the door. He didn't want anyone snooping around the place and felt if he fully reopened the room so soon after his daughter's death, people may ask questions.

The next unusual occurrence on the grounds of Loftus Hall came a few days later. One of the groundskeepers was busy cleaning up after his day's work in the gardens, when he spotted something disturbing at the Tapestry Room windows.

Walking by with the last of the equipment, the fresh sea air filling his lungs, he glanced to his right. To his amazement, he saw a woman standing in the room looking back at him. He dropped what was in his hands and slowly made his way over to investigate. Wondering who it was because everyone on the estate knew no one was allowed in that room.

Getting closer, his blood ran as cold as the air around him. There standing before him was young Anne Tottenham, her beautiful face was saturated with tears however upon seeing him, a slight smile etched its way across her pale, beautiful face.

"Lady Tottenham?" he called out, just a few feet from the glass between them.

She placed her right hand upon the glass, which was followed with a slight nod from the ghost of Anne Tottenham. She removed her hand, turned, and stepped back into the shadows of the room before he could reach the window.

Staring inside, all traces of her were gone, although the room had three large windows it was still shrouded in quite a lot of shadow. So much so he could not see anything past the foot of the bed.

Panic swept over him and he raced into the house. Running down the corridor, he turned and instantly latched onto the Tapestry Room door handle. Turning it, the door didn't budge.

"Hello," he said knocking on the doors before him.

There was no response.

"Hello, Lady Anne?" he called out again, repeating

the knocking even heavier on the doors.

"What the hell do you think you are doing?" Charles roared, descending the stairs behind the bewildered man.

"I'm sorry sir but I saw her," he said, looking towards the floor.

"Saw who?" he snapped back at him, "And who do you think you are banging on my doors like that?"

The servant made no attempt at a response, he was shivering more at the thought of Charles's wrath.

"Answer me!" Charles ordered, shoving the man about like a piece of dirt.

Silence fell between the pair.

"Look at me damn it and answer my question!"

Somehow the terrified worker managed to lift his head to meet Charles' eyes, "Now tell me what you think you are doing!"

"I saw Anne," he managed to stutter.

Charles's eyes widened, "What?"

"I swear sir. I was working outside, and I saw her standing at the window, she was crying."

"What a load of God damn nonsense, and you

think you have the right to just come in here and start beating on any door you see fit?"

"I'm sorry. I didn't know what to do," he replied, once again lowering his head to the floor.

"Just finish what you were doing outside, collect your belongings, and leave!" Charles snarled.

"But I didn't-"

"What the hell did I just say?" Charles spat.

The man did as instructed and left the grounds with no idea where he was going to find another job.

Meanwhile, Charles unlocked the doors and stepped into the room where Anne had perished to investigate what the fuss was about. Stepping inside, there was no one screaming or running towards the door in a frenzy to attack him. All was quiet.

Walking over to the windows, he watched as the man he had just expelled make his way towards the gate.

"Damn idiot, people like him make me sick. Good riddance!"

Out of nowhere, Charles eyed a white figure move behind him in the reflection. Spinning, he found the room to be empty.

What is going on here? He thought, stepping into the centre of the room, the sense of being watched overcame him, as the coldness surrounding him intensified.

A gentle breeze entered the room and weaved its way along the walls, causing Anne's old clothing to dance. Suddenly, the wardrobe doors flung open, causing Charles to race for the doors and relock them firmly into position.

Having no time to catch his breath, a sinister, male laugh echoed from upstairs. The mocking became so loud he had to shield his ears and then out of nowhere came the word "Pathetic," then all was once again silent.

"Who's there?" Charles roared, trying his best to sound undeterred by the eerie events unfolding around him. However, the look on his face portrayed the fear which was storming through his body.

No reply came so Charles took a deep breath and stepped towards the main staircase. Placing a hand upon the large bannister, he glanced towards the top of the stairs and it was at that very moment his jaw hit the floor.

Stepping down towards him was the dark stranger in the same attire he had worn when he first set foot within Loftus Hall. Charles eyed the evil smirk which always made him feel uncomfortable.

"What the hell are you doing here, get out of my house," Charles spat.

The stranger's grin grew wider.

"How did you get in here? Get out before I put you out!" Charles continued pointing to the floor beneath him, trying to assert his dominance.

The stranger stretched out his arms and erupted into convulsions of laughter. "You couldn't get rid of me even if you tried. You've no idea what you are facing here do you? You killed your daughter Charles."

"What?" Charles stuttered wide eyed.

"I never left Charles, I see and know everything. You locked her away and let her starve to death. What kind of father does that unless he has something to hide?" He lowered his arms to his side "And I know what you're hiding," he said, getting closer to the man at the bottom of the stairs.

Charles, dumbfounded didn't know how to react. He couldn't rationalise what was happening in front of him or how the *man* had gained access to his home. Panic began to weave its way into the fear coursing through him.

"I don't know what you mean."

"Of course you do Charles. Tell me, do you think Anne will ever rest in peace after what you did to her?"

"Get out!" Charles said, starting up the stairs.

The dark stranger erupted into a sadistic laugher once more while he glared at Charles coming towards him.

Instantly, Charles felt a pressure push against his body. The ground floor doors began to rattle about around him as the force became stronger. Out of nowhere came a gushing wind down the stairs, past the stranger and hit Charles head on stopping him in his tracks. Latching onto the handrail, clothes flapping in the wind, he turned to the dark stranger.

"Who are you?" Charles stuttered, a ringing beginning to fill his ears.

No response came, just an unsettling stare, followed by a dismissive head shake. "You'll never get rid of me," he said as Charles had to turn his face downwards due to the pain building inside his head.

Seconds later, there was a loud clap, like the night he had left the Hall. Looking upwards, the man was gone, the ringing had stopped, and he was able to stand to his feet with no difficulty.

"Charles is everything okay? I heard you

shouting." Jane said, opening the door on the middle floor which led to their bedroom.

"Yes, everything is fine," Charles replied, trying to regain his composure.

"You sure, it sounded like you were arguing with someone?"

"Jane, I said everything is fine didn't I? Go back to bed!" he said, irritated by his wife's bombarding questions.

Jane didn't argue and slammed the door and kicked herself for bothering to see how he was in the first place.

Charles sat down on the stairs and held his head in his hands. In his mind, he replayed what he had experienced but he could come to no rational explanation. He couldn't put what he witnessed down to trickery of the mind, nor could he believe anyone could just walk in and out of Loftus Hall as they pleased. He also could not figure out how the secret about Anne's incarceration had been exposed.

He pulled himself to his feet and decided he needed a strong whiskey to help him think about what he had just been through.

The embers still flickered within the fireplace in the Card Room as Charles set a candle on top of the mantelpiece. Bottle and glass in hand, he walked over and snatched the curtain to the floor, revealing the large hole concealed behind it.

Sitting at the table beneath the damaged ceiling, he poured himself a stiff drink. There before him was the fundamental evidence of what happened on the night when he was a part of the most memorable card game ever played in Loftus Hall. *I should have never let you into this house,* he thought, taking a huge gulp of whiskey. Suddenly, the candle flame struggled to stay alight.

"You won't get to me you know," Charles said, turning and smiling towards it. "No one gets to me," he whispered slowly, taking another sip, thinking about what he had done to his daughter.

Glancing around the pulsating darkness, he turned his attention back to the gaping hole.

"Come on then, do something. You think you can drive me out of my own house? That'll never happen. I don't play foolish mind games. I'm here now so do something," he taunted, the alcohol helping his confidence.

However, no one jumped at him from the shadows. His only company was an eerie silence and the subtle creaks about the Hall as it cooled after all the open fires during the day.

"Well if you think I'm going to waste my time worrying about you, you can think again. I've more important things to be doing," Charles said, finishing his whiskey and then poured another.

In some way he thought by sitting defiantly on his own, taunting the force at work within the house, he was showing it he wasn't afraid, even though his hands were rattling and the hairs on his head where struggling to maintain their colour.

Time crawled by as the candle light died in the room. Charles had been sitting at the table for at least an hour and a half before he decided to give in and venture to bed. Pulling the door behind him, he glanced to his left towards the Tapestry Room with an uneasy sense of being watched. He quickly dragged his attention away from the large doors, and he made his way upstairs.

Climbing into bed beside his wife, he pondered how he could make what he had witnessed stop.

The rain and harsh winds beat against the old, cold, grey walls of Loftus Hall. Several days had passed since Charles' unsettling experience and his nerves still weren't the better of it.

He had travelled to the nearby village of Fethard on Sea to discuss a business deal with another local property owner, leaving Jane in the shelter of the Grand Hall. He had left in the early hours of the morning, Jane had decided to rest further.

Upon pulling herself from the grand, large bed, she decided to bathe before starting her day of *I'm better than you* about the house amongst the servants.

Wearing a thin, white dressing gown, Jane sat in front of the dressing table with a large mirror perched on top of it brushing her hair.

Daydreaming into the glass, suddenly something caught her eye behind her. Focusing her attention, it seemed to be moving.

"What the…" she said, turning in anger at the thought someone had just walked into her room without permission.

To her astonishment no one was there. Confused, she turned back to the glass to witness the white mist become thicker and closer behind her. Turning sharply, once again nothing could be seen moving about the room.

Without any time to process her thoughts, the bedroom door slowly creaked open to her left. At that moment, Jane didn't know what was colder, the icy chill running through her or the cold handle on the hair brush she was holding.

Turning back to her reflection, the eerie mist had vanished. Her jaw open she placed the hairbrush back onto the dressing table. She twitched quickly upon hearing a creaking noise in the distance. Collecting herself, she slowly made her way to the door wondering what was happening.

She peeked outside, however nothing caught her eye, but the strange creaking continued. Determined not to let any servant see her in such an alarmed state, Jane took a deep breath and stepped out into the hall.

The only thing present was the irritating noise.

Making her way down the corridor, she turned and ventured out onto the middle floor landing, connected to the ground floor via the beautifully crafted main staircase. No servant was present, nor could the source of the sound be determined, however she deciphered that it was coming from downstairs.

Slowly reaching the bottom of the stairs, she was drawn to the Tapestry Room. Placing her ear slowly to the door, her eyes widened, she had identified where the noise was coming from.

After hearing Charles' warnings to the workers and their strange claims about the room, she rationalised someone had gone in and was nosing about the place.

She tried the door handle, it turned, but the door

wouldn't budge. Bewildered, she quickly went back upstairs hoping Charles had left key to the room in his coat pocket from the day before. Searching, she found it, and raced back down to the Tapestry Room.

You're going to be in serious trouble when I get you, she thought, inserting the key and quickly turning the lock to the open position. Shoving open the door, she was greeted by a heavy silence.

Stomping into the room, no one could be seen. Confused, Jane looked behind the door, sure that she was going to find a person cowering behind it, but nothing. The dubious noise sounded once more from the far side of the room.

Coward must be in the wardrobe, sped into her mind, as she raced over and swiped open the doors. The splashes of rain beat against the glass beside her whilst the heavy, overcast sky cocooned the land. Again Jane found nothing out of the ordinary, just some of Anne's old dresses unceremoniously flung about their hangers.

The creaking sound came once again, only this time it was behind her and accompanied by soft sobbing. Jane quickly turned, and her eyes lit up with horror identifying what was causing the sounds. Before her on the floor, sitting in the exact same position where she had died was Anne Tottenham rocking back and forth. Jane's face grew paler by the second watching Anne's head rise and turn towards her. The rocking stopped and the smile widened.

Jane turned and darted for the door which slammed shut in front of her with a deafening wallop. She had to put her hands out in front of her to prevent her crashing face first into it.

"You let me die in here," Anne said in a hoarse tone.

Hearing the voice behind her, Jane's teeth began to chatter. Lowering her hands from the door, she slowly turned.

"You let me die in here and helped cover it up!" Anne roared at her.

Jane was dumbfounded and couldn't form any sort of reaction as she witnessed a woman speak to her from beyond the grave.

Without any warning, Anne ran towards her in a flurry of pure rage. Watching the spectre advance towards her, Jane erupted into a fit of shrieks. She closed her eyes, fell to the ground and clenched her fists in front of her face waiting for the bombardment to begin, when suddenly the door pushed open behind her.

"What on earth is going on in here?" Jane opened her eyes, Anne was gone, and in walked Charles.

"Why are you in here?" he said helping her back to her feet.

"I saw her," the petrified woman said, laying into his arms.

"Who?"

"Your daughter Charles, I saw Anne. She was here," she said, as she sobbed into his shoulder.

Charles didn't respond. He couldn't find the words to comfort her. He quickly glanced around the room looking for any sign of his dead daughter's presence, but all was as should be. He cast his mind back to the experience he had a few nights before and was horrified at the thought of the developing strange occurrences in the house.

"Come on, let's get you out of here," he said, guiding the trembling woman to the doorway.

In the hallway, they were greeted by chaos. The beautiful flowers, which were picked from the fine gardens and placed in vases throughout the Hall, were thrown about the floor and torn bed sheets were blatantly tossed about the banisters of the stairs.

"What's happening Charles?" Jane asked.

"I don't know," he said, taking in the unbelievable sight in front of them. "Come with me."

He guided her out to the Coach House and instructed the workers to remain with her. Charles rounded up others to accompany him back into the house to tidy up and see if any explanation could be obtained.

Of course, the individuals he picked for the task weren't keen on going into the house after all the rumours circulating about the place. Charles noticed that less and less people would spend anytime within the walls of Loftus Hall, opting to complete works outside instead.

Re-entering the home, Charles and the others were greeted with a vile, nauseating odour which seemed to intensify as they made their way through the house. Stepping passed the back servant staircase, they slowly made their way down the long, dark corridor. Charles told them to be prepared for anything, but they didn't know what to fear the most – what he was afraid of or what he would have done if they had refused to go in with him. Turning left, they walked through the door into the large open space, filled with unique hand carvings and the awe-inspiring staircase, most of which now was unceremoniously covered with sheets, clay, or broken flowers. More disturbances seemed to have occurred since he had left the building. Pews where tossed over, candles flung to the ground, and the smell which permeated their nostrils, was strongest at the foot of the stairs. It looked like a tornado had ripped through the place and a foreboding darkness seemed to be trying to extinguish the natural light.

"Okay get cleaning," Charles instructed, keeping an eye on the upper floor, he couldn't shake the overwhelming feeling of being observed by something above them.

The men did as instructed and started gathering up the mess. Only moments had passed when strange noises could be heard from upstairs. The workers all paused and looked towards Charles, who had a look on his face which needed no explanation, they nervously continued the clean-up.

Meanwhile, Charles surveyed the top of the stairs and upper floor for any sign of movement. To him, it sounded like someone was walking about above them. Repositioning one of the pews, he sat upon it and turned his attention back to the servants tidying up in front of him.

What the hell is happening here? There has to be a simple explanation to all of this! He thought, however deep down he knew something unnatural was at work within the thick, cold walls around him.

Again, the sounds came from upstairs and the workers stopped what they were doing and stared, each trembling, looking towards the top of the stairs.

Seconds later, one of the doors, which was out of sight, slowly creaked open. This was followed by the sound of movement on the floor boards on the landing above them.

Standing to his feet, Charles listened as the disembodied footsteps made their way to the left-hand side of the landing and began their descent towards the centre of the grand stairs. Reaching the middle of the divide at the top of the staircase, the footsteps ceased.

Every individual on the ground floor looked on gobsmacked after witnessing an invisible presence move through the Hall that seemed to be observing them from the top of the stairs.

Each one of the workers wanted to drop everything and make for the nearest door, however fear had them rooted in place. One of the workers turned to Charles, whose jaw was almost touching the floor, for advice.

Seeing the opportunity, Charles turned to the help and nodded him in the direction of the stairs. The worker's eyes widened with terror.

"Go on," Charles instructed with a hand swipe.

The man, turned to the others who were looking at the floor beneath them. Turning to the main staircase, he released a huge sigh and began to climb the steps.

Each step seemed to be a mile high as he climbed closer and closer to the unknown presence in front of him. Both Charles and the rest of the workers gathered at the foot of the stairs, staring on to see what was stalking them.

Reaching the last step, the servant stood and looked around the landing. The door which had creaked open was the one which led to the bedroom of the Lord and Lady of the house, but nothing else seemed to be out of place. He waved his hand about in front of him and felt no resistance, nothing but air.

"Well?" Charles said.

"Nothing," the man replied. "Nothing is here,"

"Come on now, we all heard it, make sure," Charles ordered.

No sooner were the words spoken, when the servant was violently flung to the ground. Doors rattled furiously around them as he screamed in agony trying to get back to his feet, only to be thrown face first to the floor again and pinned firmly into position.

Two other workers raced to his aid however they were paralysed with fear eyeing a dark, pulsating figure standing at the hand rail to their left on the middle floor, watching them.

Charles spotted their faces and turned to see what they were witnessing. The human like figure had no distinguishing features, not even a face. It stood there watching the chaos it was creating.

"What do you want?" Charles roared.

The doors began to slam wildly, creating a thunderous, deafening noise.

Within seconds, the Hall fell silent, the dark figure was gone, and the battered worker was pulling himself gingerly back to his unsteady feet.

"Keep this quiet do you hear me?" Charles snarled to the workers. "If I hear one story about this outside these walls you'll all be fired," he threatened, turning towards the man walking down the stairs, aided by the two others. Still holding his chest, Charles told the servants to bring him outside and say that he *fell* if anyone asked what happened.

Meanwhile, he got the others to clean up as best they could, each keeping a close eye and ear on the floor above them.

An hour later, Charles sent word for Jane to be brought back inside while he waited for her in the Morning Room.

"How are you feeling now?" he asked, as she took a seat opposite him.

"Still a little rattled, we need to do something about this."

Charles knew she was right. A dark entity seemed to be a work within the grand Loftus Hall and he knew they would need help to try expelling it.

"I know dear I agree, but what are we going to do? This isn't exactly something we can just throw money at is it?"

"Well I don't think it's just going to go away."

"I'll work something out, don't you worry," Charles replied with as much confidence he could muster. "For now, we just need to keep a lid on this!"

This however was a task which would prove to be easier said than done. Rumours of the strange goings on and the evil which was stagnating the Hall quickly ran riot among the workers on the estate. It didn't take long for the majority of them to abstain from working inside the grand, cold walls, for fear of encountering what lurked inside. Inevitably Charles lost his temper with each one of them and spat them off the site quicker than they could catch a second breath. After about a week of firing, Loftus Hall was left with a skeleton crew of overworked individuals who did their utmost to remain at work outside on the Hall grounds.

Eventually the last of the help left their roles when

late one night one of the gardeners witnessed a large, dark figure slowly walk about the top floor of the Coach House amongst the others sleeping. Peering out from beneath her blanket, aided by the sliver of moonlight, she watched it stop, turn, and stare right at her. Paralysed with fear, she witnessed the entity turn and then slowly made it's way back down the wooden stairs. Upon hearing her account the following morning, the rest of the workers left Loftus Hall without announcing their departure.

Charles and Jane were left in a large, luxurious Hall alone. For the first time for as long as he could remember, Charles had no one at his disposal to command as he saw fit. He was Lord of a silent Hall which would quickly fall into disorder if he didn't find a solution to the infection working its way through it.

Over the next number of evenings, Charles sat in one of the grand, expensive furniture ridden rooms, with plenty of whiskey in hand. He spent countless hours bouncing thoughts around his head pondering what he was going to do, rather how he was going to redeem his and the Hall's former glory. *After all a man's power comes from the control and dominance he has over others,* he thought. When Jane slept at night, the silence of the Hall became deafening. He felt as though he was slowly being broken down by the silent malevolence monitoring his downfall.

"Why don't you just show yourself, come on!" he slurred. "I'm not afraid of you anymore," he mocked, taking another sip of the potent beverage in his hand.

Nothing.

"Hiding in shadows, hiding from me!" he continued, stumbling to his feet. "Come on, do your worst. You won't make me leave my own home," Charles roared into the night.

Suddenly, a breeze entered the room causing the candle flame to flick about on the wick. A stagnant smell of rotten meat filled the air causing the gag reflex on the man of the house to react. Suddenly darkness enveloped him. Not like the night, but a thick heavy, pressing darkness filled the room causing the candle light within to struggle to hold it at bay. Without warning, the table beside the nauseated man emitted a crushing thud, as if someone had slammed their fist upon it, causing him to spill back into his seat. He was being mocked and felt more vulnerable than ever knowing he was the only man in the house. Peering towards the door, which he had planned on darting through towards his bedroom, he eyed a tall dark figure step back into the shadows. Instantly, he burst into tears, his mind had finally broken.

Seconds later, Jane pushed past the door.

"Charles, oh God Charles are you okay? I could

hear you upstairs."

"I can't take this anymore. I'm losing my mind in this place," he said, as Jane cradled him in her arms.

Jane responded by trying to comfort him further.

"Why can't you just leave us alone?" Charles roared upward, "Just get out, LEAVE US ALONE!"

Jane spent the remainder of the night sitting with her dethroned husband, listening to each deafening creak and movement in the house, waiting for someone to lunge out from the darkness.

The following morning, as the sun broke through the darkness of the night before, Jane said "This has to end Charles. We are imploding in this place!"

"I'm going to see someone today," he returned, rubbing his unrested eyes.

The reality of the situation had finally hit him square in the face and he knew he would have to seek help, to try and reclaim his dignity and his life. Asking for help was something he had never had to do before now.

"Who?" Jane returned.

"Don't worry I'll get it sorted."

"Can I come with you? I don't like being alone in this place now."

"No, this is something I have to do alone. Why don't you go for a walk along the beach until I return. I promise we'll be okay," Charles replied, placing a hand on hers.

Jane agreed to the proposition and waved Charles away as he made the long walk down the avenue towards the main entrance. Turning back to the Hall, he hoped he could grasp the life and control he once had.

After making his way to the nearest Protestant church, Charles met with the minister inside. He explained the recent events in full detail to the minister and was amazed to hear the words, "I'm sorry, I can't get involved with anything like this Lord Tottenham."

"Do you know who the hell I am?" Charles barked back to him.

"Yes of course I do, who around here doesn't? But you see, I can't be associated with anything remotely close to this nature. It would have drastic consequences on the community."

"We can keep it quiet, just a simple prayer or something is all I need!" The Lord of Loftus Hall replied trying to clutch onto any snippet of hope he had left. He had fallen a long way from the high stature he had built for himself.

"No I'm sorry. I can't."

"Damn you. Damn you!" Charles spat back with a sinking feeling in his stomach, knowing he was losing everything. "So that's it, we just go back and try and live in an evil place like Loftus Hall without any help? We may as well just burn the place eh?"

An awkward silence fell between the pair.

Then the minister took a step forward, "Look, my hands are tied but there may be someone who can help you."

Charles made eye contact with the holy man again.

"He is a Catholic priest named Broaders and operates underground churches, so to speak, in the area. Obviously, in the times we live in, he can't be seen promoting the Catholic faith openly due to the risks of doing so, however a select few do know about his activities and whereabouts around here."

"My own church won't help me so I've to go to another for aid looking like a complete fool?"

"Trust me Lord Tottenham, if everything you have told me is true, you'd be a fool not to go and see him. However, this conversation never took place okay?"

In a desperate state of mind, Charles shook hands and agreed to never speak about his visit to the minister. He followed directions given to him in search of his now only hope, Father Thomas Broaders. Making his way to the tiny run-down cottage in Fethard On Sea, Charles felt smaller than the people he used to employee seeking help from a man of another faith. Reaching the door, he tapped his knuckles against it, but there was no reply. He tapped them against the old, battered door once again.

"Who is it?" came a voice from deep inside.

Charles thought the priest must always be on edge each time someone arrived at his door and was getting ready to dart from the back of the house.

"Don't worry, I'm not here for any trouble," Charles replied.

"That's what they all say. I asked who you are?" the voice said a little louder.

"I'm Lord Charles Tottenham and I need your help," he said, with a vulnerable feeling he had never experienced before. Help was one thing Charles thought he would never have to ask for.

Moments later, the door slowly squeaked open.

"You alone?" the priest asked. He wore no priest's

collar for fear of being caught practising the Catholic faith.

"Yes, I am."

Quickly scanning the area the priest opened the door and directed Charles inside.

"So, the great Charles Tottenham is looking for help? Yes, I've heard of you, you own almost everything around here don't you," the priest smirked.

Charles bit his tongue, knowing the man who stood before him was his only hope of banishing the unwanted presence in the Hall.

"So what can I do for you? I'm Father Broaders by the way. Decided to convert to Catholicism? I don't know if we could fit that ego of yours in here though."

"No, I need you to bless my house," Charles said, finding it unbelievable to be requesting such a thing.

The priest's eyes widened slightly.

"What?"

"You heard me."

"Get out."

"What do you mean get out, you have to help me," Charles said, raising his voice slightly.

"Listen, the only reason I let you in was to witness the almighty Charles Tottenham in person and I was slightly intrigued with how I could help you, however I'm not going to stand here and be mocked," the holy man replied firmly.

Charles wanted to reply with his usual, anger filled insults, however he needed the priest to help him regain his self-right to do so to people.

"I'm not here to mock you, I really do need your help. I need you to rid Loftus Hall of the evil inside it," he said in a soft tone.

"Don't you have your own minister?" the priest asked.

"He wants nothing to do with it."

Charles went on to explain to Father Broaders everything that had been going on recently and that he was now his only hope of regaining any form of normal life.

"It'll cost you!" the priest said, hearing and witnessing the despair in the man before him.

"What do you mean?"

"Well I'm not just going to put my neck out on the line for you, you know. Your church wants nothing to do with you and in order for me to help there has to be something in it for me. After all, it has to be worth my effort" Broaders said, preying on the weakened man before him.

Not having much choice Charles wilted, "Okay, what do you want?"

"Well, you do have loads of that fine land don't you. How about releasing your ownership over some of it," the priest grinned.

"Some man of faith you are, I can't believe what I'm hearing."

"Well, you're the one who came to me," Father Broaders smiled. "You can leave now,"

"Okay it's a deal but on one condition, this stays strictly between us," Charles surrendered.

"Wouldn't have it any other way," the priest said, hand out before him to seal it with a hand shake.

A deal was made between the pair. Father Broaders would come and bless Loftus Hall and in return he would receive three plots of land for his efforts.

Charles returned home later that day and informed Jane of what had happened and how they had been abandoned by their minster.

"A priest? Do you think he could help?" his wife asked.

"I'm willing to try anything at this stage. Whatever has wormed its way in here needs to be forced out."

"I agree, and I think it's a good idea," Jane said, placing her hand on his.

"I don't want any of this getting out, we have a reputation to keep," Charles said in a firm tone, knowing that such stories may damage the status he had created.

"You can count on me, I'll do anything I can to help."

"I know dear, let's hope he can help us put an end to it once and for all."

Later that evening, Charles sat upon the bed thinking of everything which recently occurred in his home. He wondered if his evil acts towards his daughter were finally catching up on him. He also wondered if the priest, who was their only salvation, would be able to banish the evil which had weaved its way into the Hall ever since the dark stranger had set foot through its doors.

Chapter 12

The following morning came bright and fresh. Charles had risen early and decided to walk about the Hall to wrestle with his thoughts. The voice in his head sounded insane, which brought him to the conclusion that Loftus Hall was now indeed haunted by what seemed to be two entities.

Charles Tottenham never believed in any of that sort of thing, however the events of recent times had quickly opened his mind to the possibility of the existence of ghosts and the like.

Thoughts bombarded his mind as he stepped up the back servant staircase, which he would have never been seen using if the servants were still on the estate, he knew why his daughter's ghost was tormenting him. In his opinion, Anne deserved everything she had suffered for challenging him. What he couldn't pinpoint was why he had been chosen to be subjected to the evil bombardment from the dark stranger.

We welcomed him into our home and gave him shelter. That's a lot more than anyone else would have done around here! He said to himself, reaching the top floor.

Sensing an eerie atmosphere and hearing subtle

187

creaks around him, Charles felt as though he wasn't alone. He wanted nothing more than to scream at the top of his lungs, "What do you want? Get out of this house!" However, he knew from experience it would do no good and he would no doubt be the subject of more mocking. Instead, he held his nerve and continued through the long corridors

Maybe it's punishment? He quickly wiped those thoughts from his mind. His actions had been justified and being the Lord of Loftus Hall meant no matter what, he was always right.

Reaching a window on the top floor, he peered out towards the horizon, taking in its beauty. He knew whatever evil was at play around him needed to be expelled and there was only one person who could help with the task, Father Thomas Broaders.

He reflected on the conversation with the priest and not one ounce of guilt passed through Charles hearing him sympathise with him for the death of his daughter, a death he allowed to freely happen.

Charles recalled what he said, "Thank you Father, I appreciate this. I'm counting on you for the sake of my other daughter too. She doesn't know any of this is going on and there is no way I would let her visit while these disturbances are occurring,"

Before he could visit Loftus Hall, Broaders told

Charles to pray for the soul of Anne, which would help her pass over to the other side and told him to pray to God to ask for assistance in banishing the malevolent entity he had spoke of. Although both men were of different religious backgrounds, Father Broaders believed the power of prayer was the best way to begin tackling the problem within the walls of Loftus Hall, and of course receive his payment for his help.

Little did the priest know, there was no chance in hell the man whom had come to him for aid was going to pray for his daughter. She had brought shame upon the family through her actions and he wasn't going to help her in any manner. He wanted rid of her stagnant presence and whatever else was lingering within those walls.

The drizzle swayed about the Hook Peninsula as Father Broaders pushed open one of the large gates leading to the ominous building in front of him the following day. Making his way forward, aided by the breeze pressing on his back, he could hear the waves slamming against the shoreline. He carried with him a black case and donned a heavy coat to help hold the dampness at bay. He felt uneasy approaching a house to help individuals of a different faith and of course nervous of what people might think if they found out about the deal between him and Charles. However, he rationalised he had made the risk worthwhile.

Walking towards the main door, he couldn't help but admire the grandeur of the structure before him, and the two eagles perched proudly on top of the roof watching all who approached.

Casting his eyes along the top row of nine windows, he eyed something in one of them. Behind the glass appeared to be a dark, pulsating mass watching him make his way closer to the door. The wind grew in the opposite direction, pushing against his face. The closer he got, the angrier the gusts became.

Father Broaders stared back at the entity, demonstrating he did not fear what was waiting for him inside. However, upon witnessing what he did, he was confident he was facing an evil force, one of which may need more than a simple blessing to expel.

Showing his determination to continue forward, the darkness vanished from the window and the winds eased.

Knocking on the door, he was greeted by Charles and Jane.

"Come in Father, would you like a cup of tea?" Jane asked, as she took the priest's coat.

"Yes please, that would be lovely."

He followed the pair into the Morning Room. Not wanting to panic the couple further, he did not mention seeing a dark mass in the window. He wanted to rid the home of evil with as little hassle as possible, so he could receive his entitled lands. However moving through the building he, as many before him, could not ignore the beautiful architecture Loftus Hall boosted.

Sitting at the table, he listened as Jane gave her accounts of the recent disturbances within the home and what happened during that unforgettable card game. Finishing his tea, Father Broaders asked to see the unfixable hole in the roof of the Card Room. Agreeing, Charles led the way.

Turning the door handle, they stepped into the cold, dark room. Charles reached and pulled the thick, heavy curtain to the ground so the priest could observe the evidence. Taking in the charred wood, he made the sign of the cross with his right hand and simultaneously the door they had just stepped through slowly closed.

"So, a lot of the strange happenings started after he left?" Father Broaders asked.

"Yes, Father and after Anne passed away too," Jane added.

"I see," he said, turning to the pair. "I think it's

going to take a little more than just a blessing to help you, judging by what I've heard,"

Instantly, fear encased their eyes as their mouths hit the floor.

"What do you mean Father?" Charles finally spouted.

"Whatever evil dwells here, I feel can only be expelled by performing an exorcism. This will also help Anne's soul to pass to the other side."

They couldn't believe their ears that such a practice was being suggested to help achieve a peaceful life.

"Isn't that only done on people?" Jane stuttered.

"Exorcism is an ancient rite which indeed is carried out on individuals who are influenced by evil, however from time to time the prayers of exorcism may be carried out on inanimate objects. When dealing with a person I need permission from my superiors to perform one. However in a case like this permission need only be granted by the owner of the object which is under the evil influence," he said, turning to Charles.

"Please get rid of whatever it is," Charles returned, with panic in his voice.

"Okay, I'm going to have to ask you to leave me

alone as I prepare, maybe go back to the Morning Room until I come for you?" the priest suggested.

Charles nodded in agreement and left with Jane as Father Broaders placed the large case he had brought with him upon the card table.

Flicking open the buttons on the case, he pulled out a vial of holy water, a purple stole with a gold cross in the middle and one at each end, and a Bible.

Gently kissing the back of the stole, he placed it over his head, around his neck, and draped it over his shoulders. Picking up the Bible and holy water, an instant chill ran its way through the room, bringing with it a growing dread. Father Broaders, Bible tucked firmly by his left side, made the sign of the cross in the centre of the room and began to pray.

A deafening silence crashed upon the house. There was no sign of the dark stranger or Anne Tottenham's ghost.

Reaching to the vial, he opened the lid and began to sprinkle the holy water about the room. Judging by what he witnessed when he approached the house earlier, and the horrid stories the Tottenham's had told him, the priest expected an immediate violent backlash from the dark entity which had attached itself to the property in an attempt to prevent him from beginning his role, however all was quiet. He pushed open the Drawing Room door and made the sign of the cross, continued praying and sprinkled the holy water into the four corners of the room. Again nothing out of the ordinary was observed.

Father Broaders carried out the exact same process in each room on the ground, middle, and third floors of the building without even a peep. However, the sense of dread he felt seemed to be growing.

Returning to the main staircase, it was time for the main prayers of the exorcism to begin. The priest felt this area was the heart of the house and knew there was no way an evil entity could withstand this portion of the rite without making its presence known.

Kneeling down on one of the steps, he placed the Bible and vial of sacred water in front of him. He then placed his palms together and begin the prayers of exorcism. Instantly, strange noises could be heard about the upstairs of the house. Undeterred, Father Broaders kept his eyelids sealed shut and continued to pray.

The darkening clouds above him swirled rapidly and the light shining through the glorious, open glass roof grew dimmer with each passing second. Still praying, he could hear a low growl growing in the distance. Determined not to show any weakness, the priest prayed even harder. The guttural snarls came from every direction around the holy man as the beautiful doors which led to the awe invoking staircase began to rattle as though they were locked, and someone was trying to get break in. Whispers began to circulate the priest's ears uttering things like,

"Get out, you're not wanted here,"

"You'll never banish me,"

"Your God doesn't exist,"

"I know about the deal you made"

"You're no better than me," and *"I'll make you leave."*

However, none of these seemed to play on the priest's mind. The growls became painfully loud, and suddenly the Bible was flung hard against the priest's chest.

Gasping for air to reflate his lungs, he opened his eyes. The house fell abruptly silent once again. Clutching his chest, Father Broaders pulled himself to his feet and looked about the banisters and the floor above him. Nothing could be seen. Suddenly the vial of holy water crashed off the man's temple instantly creating a huge gash on his skin. As he placed pressure on the wound, the blood flowed down the back of his hand. Stumbling in pain, an evil laughter erupted and the word "Pathetic," was heard in the Great Hall.

The priest's mouth hung in disbelief taking in the

blackest of shadows standing before him at the top of the stairs. The dark stranger was making himself known. Expecting further confrontation, the man quickly reached for the Bible and placed it before him like a shield.

"In the name of Jesus Christ our Lord and saviour, I command you to leave this house!"

The dark entity advanced.

"In the name of Jesus Christ our Lord and saviour, I order you to leave at once!" Father Broaders said, raising his voice even more.

The evil kept approaching the man of God, seemingly unaffected by his commands.

"I am a servant of God and you will obey me. I order you to leave this place at once," the priest roared, followed by the sign of the cross.

Instantly, the priest was shoved forcefully backwards and he hit the floor with a violent thud. The house fell silent once again and the evil presence disappeared back into the shadows it came from, however Father Broaders had not finished the prayers, therefore the exorcism was incomplete. He knew now that exorcising Loftus Hall was going to be a very tough task indeed.

Regaining his composure, he turned and went back

to the rattling couple who were awaiting an update in the Morning Room.

"I think it's best if you stay out of the house tonight," the priest said, wiping the blood and sweat from his brow, still holding his aching chest. "Maybe stay out in the Coach House until all of this is over."

Charles couldn't believe the words being thrown at him. Never in a million years had he considered ever staying where the help used to stay.

"What do you mean, haven't you gotten rid of it?" Charles asked, standing to his feet, ignoring the man's obvious wounds.

"No, we are dealing with a very powerful force here. It's going to take all my faith and prayer to banish this evil and it's best you and your wife are not here to get caught in the middle of it."

"We're already in the middle of it Father. What the hell is it anyway?" the man snapped back.

"I don't know, but whatever it is, isn't going to leave without a fight," the holy man returned, even though he had a fair idea who had infested the Hall, however he didn't want to cause further panic among the occupants.

"Come on Charles, let's do as he asks. He is only trying to help," Jane said, clutching his arm.

Spotting her fear, Charles surrendered to the suggestion made by Father Broaders and ventured out to the Coach House. Making their way upstairs, Charles never felt as little in his life. Meanwhile, inside the thick, grey walls of Loftus Hall, Father Broaders tended to his wound and prepared to go to war once again with the malevolent force that lurked within the long corridors.

Striking a match, he swung the flame over to each of the candle holders on the main staircase. Once the two were throwing out their light, he fell to his knees once more on the hard wooden steps and lit a candle standing proudly in its holder on the stairs in front of him. He retrieved another vial of holy water and a crucifix from his case. The rain patted against the glass above his head as he began to recite the prayers which had gained him his recent injuries. Keeping his eyelids firmly stitched together, he made his way past the first number of lines unhindered, however the unusual creaking sounds, like timber flooring under pressure, emanating from the building around him, hinted to him he may be in for round two sooner than he thought.

"They left me in here," floated from the room to his left, undeterred Father Broaders' attention remained fixed on the delivery of prayer.

"To…die," a voice sounded to his left once more.

Without a moment to process the words and where they were coming from, the Tapestry Room doors slowly creaked open beside him. Again, the priest kept his concentration on the Lord and saviour and the prayers granted to him.

A cool chill made its way around his body as the sounds echoed from upstairs. Spinning to the two large doors, for the first time, the priest caught sight of the apparition of Anne Tottenham. She wore a long, flowing white and blue dress and looked as stunning as she did long before she had slipped into her pit of insanity.

"Anne?" Father Broaders said, standing to his feet, collecting the candlestick holder from the stairs, then he stepped quickly to the doors.

As he did, he watched Anne retreat into the murky shadows of the Tapestry Room.

"Anne?" he called once more, pushing open the door.

Peering into the blackness, nothing could be seen except the flickering shadows cast from the bland furniture inside. Seconds later, he heard the sounds of footsteps behind him. Turning, he eyed Anne walking up the grand staircase. Sobbing uncontrollably, she reached the top, turned to him, then vanished.

Spinning on his heels, Father Broaders tossed holy water into the Tapestry Room and quickly closed the doors behind him.

"May you rest in peace Anne, leave this place and move onto your reward in paradise," he said, taking his place at the foot of the stairs once more.

"May the evil that dwells within this house be forced out by the love of our Lord and God," the priest said at the top of his voice holding the crucifix aloft. "I command you to leave this place."

There was no response, only the rain slamming against the glass overhead.

"By the authority of Jesus Christ, I order you to go back to where you came from, never to return again," he said, in a more assertive tone.

Moments passed, and a mocking laughter could be heard as though it came from the house itself.

"God? Jesus Christ?" hissed in the priest's ears. "You really think they can banish me?"

Father Broaders was suddenly overcome with a nauseating feeling and vomited the entire contents of his stomach all over the stairs.

Swiping the sick from the side of his mouth, it was then he felt the heavy breathing on the back of his neck. Turning, he took in the sight of the cloven hoofed dark stranger standing there in all his smirking glory.

"Who are you?" asked the fear-stricken man.

"Oh I think you know who I am priest, now let's see if you can enforce your feeble threats. You're not even here purely to help, you took payment for this. You and I have a lot in common. I have taken their power and you their land," he laughed.

"In the name of-"

The fiend in front of the man of faith erupted into a fit of mocking laugher, quickly accompanied by a horrendous clap of thunder. All candle light died.

Moments later, Father Broaders struggled with shaking hands and finally succeeded in relighting the candle beside him and to his relief the beast was gone. He was toying with the man of God.

For the reminder of the night, Father Broaders prayed unhindered at the foot of the staircase, the heart of the house, opting not for exorcism prayers, but rather other blessings until he regained some of his strength.

The following morning came with a dull, thick overcast sky. The holy man had not slept the entire night and was somewhat relieved to see the weak daylight try forcing its way through the clouds over the glass above him. Suddenly, three loud thumps echoed from the front door. Pulling himself to his feet, the priest made his way through the Card Room to the Main Hall. Opening the doors, he was greeted by Charles and Jane.

"So is it done?" the man of the house immediately quizzed.

"I have a little more to do I'm afraid, and until then I don't want anyone to come into this house."

A huge sigh and a look of dissatisfaction was the response.

"I'm going to have to spend more time here today to finish the exorcism to ensure it has been effective."

"Well, why don't you get back to work then? Don't forget what I gave you to do this," Charles said in a dismissive tone, wondering what was taking so long.

"Let the man get some breakfast first. He looks like he hasn't had any rest at all," Jane said, smiling to the man who was trying to banish the evil from Loftus Hall.

"Ok come out and join us," Charles instructed.

Father Broaders didn't let Lord Tottenham's coldness bother him. After all, the man wanted things to return to normal in the house as soon as possible.

After finishing an unusually bland Tottenham guest breakfast in the Coach House, Father Broaders gave his thanks and ventured back to the huge house once more.

Stepping towards the Hall, the wind began to pick up across the countryside. Taking in the ominous building, on his way back inside its walls, he knew he was facing a tough battle ahead and wondered if he would be the one who would come out as the victor.

Closing the door behind him, an instant sense of dread came over him once more and he felt as though there were a thousand eyes watching his every movement. He began as the day before by blessing all the rooms in the building once again with holy water. Fetching the Bible, he decided to walk about the Hall while he carried out the rite. Starting up the back staircase, he held the Bible tightly to his chest and began reciting the prayers of exorcism. Almost instantly, he felt a pressure on his lungs. Pressing upwards, Father Broaders began to see dark shadows in the corner of his eye, moving about the grand, long dark corridors, watching him. Reaching the third floor, the priest made his way down the lengthy top hallway to the furthest room.

"Lord bless this place, cleanse this place, and rid it of all evil," the man said, before he began into the next phase of the exorcism.

As he began the prayers, he could hear items smashing in the distance. Each one of them fiercely crashing to the floor in sequence. The tirade made its way to the third floor and peering down the corridor, he witnessed each beautiful ornament levitate and slam to pieces by an unseen force. The door before him crashed shut and then silence. He continued with the prayers as a stagnant smell of rotting flesh filled his nostrils almost causing him to vomit as he had done the day before.

His anxiety growing, Father Broaders was flung hard against the wall by the fiend who clearly didn't appreciate God's prayers being spoken about the house. Determined not to allow the evil to get the better of him again, Father Broaders began to say the Our Father aloud with solid commitment. Eyes closed, held in place by the back of his neck, he heard profanity and mockery whispered into his ear through gritted teeth, however he continued praying, clutching the Bible to his chest as hard as possible.

"You'll never rid this place of me priest, I am eternal."

"Amen," the prayer was finished, and the priest was alone in the room.

Stiff with pain, he slowly rounded his head on his shoulders while rubbing the area where an unbreakable grip had held him in place. Father

Boarders gingerly made his way back down to the ground floor, all the time accompanied by creaking floor boards and subtle knocks behind him. Once again, the expelling rite had been interrupted by the force that dwelled within the grand walls around him. It was at that moment he wondered if the spirit of Anne Tottenham was haunting Loftus Hall willingly or if she was trapped within the walls by the same malevolence which was testing the man's spiritual strength.

Swinging open the Tapestry Room doors, he walked inside.

"Anne, you can rest in peace now, there is nothing more here for you," he repeated, sprinkling droplets of holy water before him, and making the sign of the cross.

"I didn't deserve to be locked in here," sobbed a voice opposite him.

Father Broaders couldn't find the source of the voice. "Anne, you can move on now, you can be at rest."

"I can't, not until my love returns," she replied to the man of faith.

It was then Father Broaders began to ponder if she knew there was another entity, a sadistic force haunting Loftus Hall alongside her. *Surely a soul as pure as hers wouldn't linger here if she knew evil dwelled here too,* he said to himself, maybe Anne was unaware of the other forces at work around her. Father Broaders decided to continue with the exorcism and hoped that once he banished the evil from the Hall, it would also help the poor young woman's soul finally find peace.

As evening fell on the Hall, Father Broaders prepared to move into the final phase of the exorcism. Using the Card Room table, from his case, he retrieved a white cloth and placed it onto the table, which sat beneath the gaping hole in the ceiling above it. Returning to the case, he pulled out a fine chalice, a bottle of sacramental wine, and a circular container which housed the Eucharist. Slightly surprised he hadn't faced any further opposition since earlier in the day, he lit the two candles, one to the left and right of him on the table and began the Mass as the rain beat against the windows beside him.

Moments after placing the Body of Christ into his mouth, the disturbances began again. A breeze from no clear origin swirled about the room causing the flames to cling onto the wicks for dear life. The priest kept his eyes closed and prayed. Suddenly a great nauseating feeling swept over him as his stomach began to churn, but he was determined to digest the host. Opening his eyes, the priest picked up the chalice and pressed it to his lips, taking a sip, he prayed and placed it back onto the table. Suddenly, a growl echoed within the room and the chalice and its contents were tossed to the floor. A pungent smell filled the air, overwhelming the holy man, and the mockery started once more.

"Stupid priest, you really think you can say a few prayers to Him and that's the end of it? I am more powerful than you know," was uttered in a guttural voice.

"In the Lord's name I command you to leave this house!" the priest roared at the evil entity.

This was followed by a loud laugh, further blasphemy, and a dark manifestation before the priest.

"You will do as instructed," Father Broaders shot back with authority, while tossing holy water at the unholy presence before him.

The swirling shadows quickly moved out of the line of fire and swiftly advanced and struck the priest across the face, leaving a huge red slap mark on his skin. Holding the stinging injury, the stunned man made the sign of the cross before him and began reciting prayer. As he did, the smell of rotting flesh grew more pungent and the doors and windows around him began to rattle violently. While praying, a voice in his head was saying the same prayer backwards, trying its utmost to put the man of faith off his goal. A calmness suddenly struck the room as the three doors around it slowly creaked open. Opening his eyes, he stepped towards the main staircase.

Walking by the Tapestry Room, its doors too slowly creaked open, however his attention was drawn to the foot of the stairs. Standing before him again was the spirit of Anne Tottenham sobbing uncontrollably.

"Anne?"

She continued to cry without looking at the priest.

"Anne, you have to leave this place now,"

"Leave me alone. You can't help me," the distraught spectre said, before disappearing.

Standing *alone* in the grand surroundings of Loftus Hall, the house seemed alive. He couldn't help but feel as though he was failing Anne and the Tottenham family, and would soon fail in achieving his payment if he didn't win the internal battle. He returned and finished the Mass waiting for another bombardment of assaults but they never came.

As night shrouded the Hall in a thick darkness, Father Broaders decided to put his head down and get some rest. The holy man was unable to get any form of sleep the entire night due to the sinister whispering, loud bangs, footsteps and furniture moving in the distance.

By the arrival of the third day, the priest was completely drained. Pulling his aching body to the side of the bed, he knew he only had one final house blessing to carry out for the exorcism to be complete. He wondered if it would have any effect on the forces at work around Loftus Hall at all. Fetching a crucifix and holy water, he began the final blessing on the house.

Working his way from top to bottom, he recited prayers paying strict attention to his surroundings. It was too quite. He was waiting for an attack at any moment.

Stepping into the Tapestry Room, he began to sprinkle the holy water and suddenly the altercation began.

"Get out of this house," growled a voice from the shadows.

"I order you to leave," the priest replied, still throwing the water about the room.

"Never!"

The holy man's ears rapidly filled with horrid shouting and a woman's cries, Father Broaders was being broken down slowly over time with every conflict in the Hall. Just before he was about to wince in pain, he broke his composure and held the crucifix before him.

"In the name of our Lord Jesus Christ, I bind whatever evil is in this house to this room. If you don't want to leave, may you never leave, this shall be your punishment. Stay here for eternity."

Father Broaders was forcefully pushed backwards. Keeping his balance, he continued,

"I bind you to this room in the name of the Father," the growling intensified, "the Son," he could hear Anne Tottenham's sobbing growing even louder, "and the Holy Spirit."

Then all was quiet, except for his shallow breathing.

"Anne," he finally said, "If you can hear me, you can leave this house. Please Anne go and be at peace, this is not the place for you."

Father Broaders glanced about the room, listening for any sign of her departure or acknowledgement but nothing could be heard, just silence. He finished sprinkling the holy water in each corner of the room before retreating into the hallway and closed the doors firmly behind him. Before the doors latched shut, he heard a growl, like a caged dog, from the darkness.

Collecting his equipment, he knew the exorcism had failed however he wondered if the binding he performed would hold the evil that had plagued Loftus Hall within the Tapestry Room forever so it couldn't further torment any other souls. Placing the items back into the suitcase, he closed it, and went back to the Coach House.

"So it's done?" Charles asked with a stern look.

"Not yet, I must collect something. But whatever you do, do not let anyone into that house until I say okay?" the priest returned.

"Okay, don't be long," Charles said with a long sigh.

Father Broaders left immediately and returned sometime later with a large, dark bag draped over his shoulders.

"This will just take a moment," he said, once again retrieving the key from Charles.

Stepping in through the front door, he turned left and passed through the Card Room out towards the marvellous main staircase. Father Broaders glanced towards the Tapestry Room momentarily wondering if something still lurked within and if Anne's spirit had finally departed the Hall. Turning, he made his way up the steps. Reaching the top, he took a moment, and then slid the straps of the bag off his right shoulder and placed it gently beside him. Stooping down, he carefully opened the bag to reveal a large wooden crucifix. Lifting it, he placed it gently into the indent in the wall at the head of the staircase, Jesus facing outward. Kneeling before it, Father Broaders prayed several minutes and then blessed himself. Rising to his feet, he turned and ventured out towards the Coach House.

"Thanks for all your help Father," Jane said, stepping onto the beautiful titled floor.

There came no response.

"What's that?" Charles asked, eyeing the latest item in the Hall.

"There is something I should tell you and you both need to take what I'm about to say very seriously," Father Broaders said.

"Okay," Charles said, eyebrows scrunched, looking sideways at the man.

"There is an extremely strong evil within this house. I managed to rid it from most of the rooms, however I could not rid it entirely as it is very powerful."

"What do you mean, we hired you to get this thing out and now you're telling me it's still here?" Charles snarled.

"There is only so much I can do. I've bound the entity to the Tapestry Room and there it shall remain for eternity. This crucifix has been blessed," the priest said turning to the large representation of Christ "I placed it in the heart of the house where it will help to keep evil at bay. Never remove it from the stairs. However, the main responsibility will remain with the people within Loftus Hall."

Charles and Jane turned to one another and then back to the man in front them.

"Do not let anyone go into that room under any circumstances, keep the doors and window shutters locked at all times. Keep a positive, happy atmosphere about the place because evil will grow stronger with negativity, and most of all have faith and pray," Father Broaders instructed. "A great evil has entered this house and here it will remain locked away in that room."

All three turned towards the Tapestry Room doors, doors which seemed to pulsate with an evil energy.

"So that's it?" Charles said, turning back to the priest.

"I'm afraid I've done all I can. Whatever is in there is stronger than you or I," Father Broaders replied in a firm tone.

"I'm sorry Father," Charles returned. "We've been so worked up these last few weeks and the last number of days have really taken their toll. Please forgive my rudeness, we both appreciate what you have done for us," Charles said, thinking he may finally be able to begin to re-establish the family name.

"Events like this can really stretch people to their limits. I do regret the exorcism wasn't a total success, however things should hopefully improve around here," the holy man said with a gentle smile.

Charles mirrored the smile and stepped over to the room which was housing a dark, malevolent force. Turning the key and hearing the latch click firmly into position. "No one will ever set foot inside that room ever again. I'll have the doors screwed shut later too."

"Would you like something to eat?" Jane asked, still processing the events of recent times.

"No thank you. I have to say Mass later, so I should go back to prepare."

Jane left the men to speak.

"Listen, take this before you go," Charles said, reaching into his fine coat pocket and pulling from it a considerable sum of money. "For your trouble."

"Thanks, and the land?" he said, collecting his

briefcase.

"Yes, don't worry, that will be sorted for you too. But remember, not a word of this, that will be a clause in the contract," Charles said, stretching out his hand to the man in front of him.

"I won't say a word. Remember no one goes in, doors and windows stay locked, the crucifix stays where it is, and most of all pray. You know where I am if you need me for anything."

The priest shook the man's hand and left the building through the front door with his reward, the front door through which the evil had entered Loftus Hall.

Reaching the end of the long avenue, Father Broaders turned back towards the commanding building dominating the landscape, stepping through the large gates, he paused and said to himself, *I do know who you are! And I pray, I, and no one else ever has to witness your evil again.*

The End.

A Glimpse Inside Loftus Hall.

The Main Staircase.

The Tapestry Room.

The Card Room.

Images supplied by Aidan Quigley.

About the Author

Chris lives in County Wicklow, Ireland. He has wrote
a number of successful horror works and strives to
make each story better than the last.

www.chrisrushauthor.com

Other Books by Chris Rush

FOLKLORE
ALL SHALL SUFFER
13 DEAD
FOLKLORE: THE SECOND TALE

For further information on Loftus Hall please visit
www.loftushall.ie